Sex Scenes

Erotica Excerpts from the Novels of Kim Corum

Also by Kim Corum:

Playtime
99 Martinis: Uncensored
Heartbreaker
Breaking the Girl
The Other Woman
Now She's Gone
Eager to Please
Dead Sexy: Two Tales of Vampire Erotica

Sex Scenes

Erotica Excerpts from the Novels of Kim Corum

by

Kim Corum

New Tradition Books

Sex Scenes: Erotica Excerpts from the Novels of Kim Corum
by
Kim Corum

New Tradition Books
ISBN 1932420630

*This book is a work of fiction. Names, characters, places and
incidents are either the product of the author's imagination or are
used fictitiously. Any resemblance to actual events or locales or
persons, living or dead is entirely coincidental.*

For information contact:
New Tradition Books
newtraditionbooks@yahoo.com

For You.

"I just had sex with another man!"
From *Playtime*.

The setup: Mona and her husband have agreed to an open relationship. In this scene, she experiences sex with another guy for the first time.

Neal, too, had decided to cook for me. He burned two NY Strip steaks to a crisp then called for a pizza. We drank a few beers, smoked a few cigarettes, all the while eyeing one another, knowing what we'd be doing later on. It was very tantalizing. It was also nerve-wracking. I was so edgy, I could have jumped right out of my skin. But then, would he put me back in?

We were out on his patio. I noticed how he kept everything very neat, even his potted plants looked healthy and vibrant with no dead leaves. Maybe I had been wrong about him. He seemed a little nervous and kept asking me if he could get me this or that. I watched with one raised eyebrow as he made a fuss over me. I tried to appear cool, though I was a nervous wreck inside.

"How about another beer?" he asked.

"No, thanks."

"Is the pizza okay?"

"Yeah," I said. "It's pretty good."

He nodded and pointed at my cigarettes. "I can run to the store for more cigarettes cause it looks like you'll be out later."

"I have another pack in my car."

"Oh, okay," he said and smiled at me, then looked up at the sky. "Oh, look at all the stars tonight. I see the Big Dipper."

I looked up too. I couldn't tell one set of stars from another, but I nodded like I could. "Oh, right."

He turned back to me. "I can turn this down if you want. You do like Sarah McLachlan, don't you?"

No, not really, I'm more of a Motorhead fan. I mean *what the fuck?* He kept chick music around? Despite that, he was a lot cooler than he had been previously. I was actually beginning to like him. Of course, he wasn't drunk off his ass like last time.

"I have some pot," he said. "If you like."

I shook my head. I didn't want to get high. I wanted to feel every second of this.

He nodded, then said, "You're very pretty."

"Thanks," I mumbled, wondering when he was going to get the show on the road.

He leaned in towards me and took my hand. My heart seemed to jump up inside of my chest and began to thump madly. I was in a nervous titter; it was almost like the first time I ever did it, like I was a virgin again. Except I'd remember most of this, if it were pleasant enough. Thankfully, it appeared to be headed in that direction.

He leaned in and brushed his lips against my cheek and breathed, "You're so beautiful."

Such a nice thing to hear when one is on a constant state of self-doubt. Gee... Thanks. You ain't too bad yourself.

"I can't believe how lucky I am."

Aw, come on. He was getting mushy. And I hated mushy.

He got out of his chair and down on his knees in front of me. He began at my hand, just soft kisses, then up my arms, my neck, my face. Then, my lips. My tongue touched his. We kissed. It was a nice kiss, a gentle kiss. Our mouths moved against each other's for a moment and then we really began to explore. The kiss was now lusty and I was panting. I got turned-on enormously just from the way he kissed me and I wanted more and more of it. I loved the way he kissed and he was a good kisser. He took his time but he was forceful, like he wasn't about to move away from me, lest the mood change.

I knew then and there he was going to be the one. He was my number two guy, the second guy I would fuck. I was so glad I had picked him. I was so glad it was about to happen.

He kept kissing me, then pulled me up and walked me backwards all the way into the bedroom. Our lips stayed on top of each others as if we couldn't get enough of this kiss. I know I couldn't. We made it into the bedroom and he laid me down on the bed, then slowly, very slowly, he undressed me.

I couldn't believe it was happening. I was about to do it. I had dreamed about this very thing for so long it seemed almost surreal, as if it were a fantasy. But it wasn't a fantasy. It was real. And it was good.

I tugged at his clothes, but he pushed my hands away. I felt, for an instant, very vulnerable, then he took off the remainder of my clothes and kissed my naked body, licked it, touched it, admired it, worshipped it.

I was squirming, groaning, panting, wishing he'd fuck me. Now! Come on! *Get in!* I was dying to see what he felt like once he was inside me. That was the part I wanted most.

I helped him get out of his pants and underwear, then pulled him back on me. And then, he put it in. I gasped a little from the pressure and the excitement was almost too much. It started slowly as we adjusted. Then more quickly, more passionately. He stopped and pulled me into his lap. I moaned in ecstasy as he kissed my chest, then my neck, back down to my breasts, then up again. He had a way with his tongue. It just slid along my skin and then would stop and suck gently, then harder.

He laid me back down on the bed again I wrapped my legs around his waist. Then it escalated. He really began to get into it. He began to forget about me. I forgot about him and used his body to make me come, like a big vibrator with lips and hands. And he was all over me, kissing, touching. I kissed, too, but before I knew what was happening, I was bucking up against him and was coming. I was so caught up in the moment I couldn't do anything but hang on for the ride. The orgasm was coming quicker than I expected. It just jumped out at me and I exploded. I felt like I burst into a thousands pieces. I shook with it and held him as close to me as I could get him and rode it out. As I came back down from it, he came, then fell on top of me, kissed my cheek, and rolled off, breathing heavily.

Oh, wow.

It dawned on me just then. I just had sex with another man. I just had sex with another man! I JUST HAD SEX WITH ANOTHER MAN! I was so excited, not just by the act itself, but by the fact that I had done it. That I was able to follow through with it. That I hadn't backed down. That I took what I wanted.

Man, that was *nice*. I took a moment to reflect. Okay, done. One, two, three, four… How long did I have to wait? I stared at him. He looked so content. I couldn't help but smile and put my arm around him and give him a little squeeze. After I did that, I moved away quickly because I really wanted to leave so I could gather my thoughts and just *feel* it for a moment before real life took over again. I figured he wanted me gone soon anyway. Wasn't that the way it worked? *Slam, bam, thank ya ma'am!*

"That was great," he muttered and snuggled up next to me.

What was this shit? I thought guys wanted you OUT OUT OUT once it was over and here he was acting like he... Like he wanted to cuddle. Sure, Clay always wanted to cuddle afterwards but I just figured he was different from most men. I hadn't expected Neal to want that, too. How odd. How very fucking weird.

"Uh huh," I muttered and kept counting...five, six, seven... Fuck it.

I pulled away and began to dress. I had to get out of there and get my head on straight before I saw Clay. And I couldn't wait to see him. Seeing him was almost as important to me as the sex had been, if not more so. Seeing him would tell me so many things, like if we were going to be able to do this, if we were going to be able to accept it. If we were going to be able to stay together.

"Where you going?" he asked.

"I've got to pick someone up."

"Excuse me?"

"Maybe we'll do this again," I said and kissed his nose. "But right now, I've got to go."

Bewildered, he watched me go. I grinned and skipped to my car.

"Sex with macho, macho man."
From *Playtime*.

The setup: Mona tests the boundaries with Hank, who happens to be Clay's best friend.

Okay, if Clay hadn't made it so obvious that I should never have Hank, I probably would have left it alone. But because he was being such an asshole, I decided to take a sick day and drive to Castile and just talk things out with Hank. I mean, I liked him and not just sexually. He made me laugh. And I didn't tell Clay a thing. Why should I?

As I drove up that old familiar road, I began to remember the excitement as the house was being framed in, though it seemed like a long time ago. How big it looked to me. How nice and new. I thought about what kind of flowers I was going to plant and what colors I would use to paint the interior. As I came to a stop in front of it, my heart did a somersault. It was two stories, blazing white and had a gigantic wrap-around porch. I should have never let Clay have it in the divorce. What did I get? My car? Our crummy furniture? Our life savings? He had this, this beautiful house.

I got out and heard a saw start in the back. I walked around and saw Hank, who was standing with his back to me, shirtless. Beads of perspiration dribbled along his perfectly tanned back. It was so muscular that when he moved, the muscles moved with him.

He just looked so damn good.

I stood there for a moment and stared at his ass, so sculpted in those jeans, which were not too tight, but not too loose. He looked like the perfect construction worker—the kind women stop and stare at and hope will give them whistles and catcalls. He must have sensed me because he turned around and gave a little wave.

"What 'cha doing?" he asked in his friendly manner.

I shrugged and stepped up on the deck. "Just thought I'd drop by.... No, that's a lie. I want to talk to you."

"About what?"

About us. About our impending affair. Our love trysts. You licking me everywhere. Me fucking you. Stuff like that. I said, "About Clay."

"Oh," he said. "Want something to drink?"

We went inside and I again cursed Clay for taking this house. Of course, he said I could have it. But it was on his father's land and I knew I'd never be happy living here if he wasn't living with me. But it was gorgeous. The sheetrock was up and all the windows installed. The kitchen cabinets—the ones I'd painstakingly picked out—were hanging beautifully in the kitchen. The stairs still needed finishing but the Jacuzzi in the master bath had been installed. In no time it would be ready to move into. I felt a lurch in my stomach. Would Clay and I move in together as originally planned? Or would he move into it by himself? Oh, God, I didn't know. This shit was driving me crazy!

I shook it off and turned back to Hank who grabbed two beers out of a tiny refrigerator, then threw the plastic off my table. Uh, Clay's table.

I began, "I don't know what Clay told you—"

"I don't want to talk about it, Mona."

"Excuse me?"

"Clay's still my best friend and he told me everything and I don't want to hear anymore."

My face stung in embarrassment.

He took a sip of beer and said, "I just don't want to be caught in the middle."

I no longer wanted to fuck him; I wanted to kill him. Give me that sledgehammer. *Now!*

I put the beer on the table and stood, deciding then and there I was one-hundred percent stupid and I hated him, Clay and the entire world. He caught me at the door.

"Get away from me," I growled.

"Mona, listen—"

"If you don't want to listen to my shit, then I don't want to listen to yours, Hank! I thought you were my friend and now you're just another asshole taking up space."

His entire face dropped all emotion. Just like that. I could have slapped him.

He muttered, "I just don't want Clay to get hurt, okay?"

"And why is that? I've already hurt him, I know. Poor Clay and his stupid ex-wife. Yeah, I know all about poor, pitiful Clay."

"Mona—"

"What do you know anyway? It's not like you even like me or anything; I'm just the asshole who drove an hour to patch things up."

"What do I know?" He stepped away from me and pointed at his chest. "I know I am the asshole who...who..."

"Who what?"

He stared at me and I got it. He liked me! He'd probably liked me for a long time! Oh, shit.

"I just can't do this, Mona," he said. "Not until you two complete whatever it you need to complete. I knew I should have just gone back to California."

"Huh?"

"I just stayed to see how long it would take..." He eyed me, as if he felt he had told too much. "Sorry. I'm talking out my ass. Just forget everything I've said."

Now how was I supposed to do that?

"It's just that Clay is such a good guy," he said. "And I want the best for him."

Anger began to simmer inside me. Clay this. Clay that. Just because I had been married to him and loved him did that mean I wasn't a whole person? Did that mean I belonged only to him and not even a tiny bit to myself? That I didn't deserve to feel things like everyone else? Did I just get that one shot? Why the fuck didn't it work both ways? *Why?!* That pissed me off because it's like he thought Clay was saying, "Your emotions, your heart, you soul belong to me." And they don't. They *BELONG TO ME!* I belong to me, not to some man. Me. That's all I am, all I'll ever be. Take it or leave it.

"Yeah, he's great," I said. "And I'm the bitch who keeps his light from shining."

"You're not a bitch, Mona."

"Yeah, I am, Hank. See ya!"

I started out the door but he stopped me. I stared up into his eyes, noticing how very gray they were. How beautiful. He had the cutest dimples, too. Straight teeth. Everything. He was a perfect man who cared more about my ex-husband than me. *Let's not step on anyone's toes or ruffle anyone's feathers.* But that's what life was about. Everything couldn't always run smoothly nor could it always be fun. There were toes that would be stepped on and feathers that would be ruffled and he couldn't change that by holding back.

"So, don't be a bitch right now, okay?" he said.

"You fucker!" I said and couldn't stop myself. Before I knew what I was doing, I had slapped him and was yelling, "Who the hell do you think you are? James Fucking Bond? Casanova? Fucking Don Juan?"

I hit him again. He let me. Then I stopped and felt kind of sick. I was really becoming unbearable to myself. And probably to everyone else in the whole world as well.

"Why'd you stop?" he asked hoarsely.

9

"Because…" I couldn't think of a reason so I just said, "I'm sorry, Hank. I don't know what's gotten into me."

"It's okay," he said as if he understood. And then he suddenly grabbed me and pulled me to him in this gigantic hug.

Oh, it felt so good to finally be in his arms without anyone else around watching. His big arms just enveloped me and made me feel so small and warm and secure.

"You're such a fiery little beast," he said.

Beast. Also known as burden. I stared up at him. I asked, "And what does that make you?"

"The asshole who loves you."

"You're full of shit."

"Come on," he said and led me back into the house. "Let's finish our beers."

We finished our beers, then another and then another. Then I was feeling better. He told me all about himself, the Navy and some other bullshit I don't care to remember. He told me jokes, sayings, stories. I told him nothing. He made me laugh so hard, I spit out my beer. I started to wipe it off of my chin but he leaned over and did it for me. His hand lingered near my mouth. I stared down at his hand and then back at him.

Swiftly, he came at me, dropping his beer in the process and I opened my arms and grabbed his face, thrusting my tongue into his mouth. He kissed me feverishly through my clothes, biting at my nipple until I thought I'd die until he took it in his mouth. He pulled my shirt over my head then sat me on the table, ripped off my jeans and buried his head between my legs, which came up and rested on his shoulders.

And everything ceased to matter. Time, space, objects. Just this touching mattered and it mattered a lot. *Ahhhh*…touch me there, run your tongue along my neck, hold me tight, never let me go. There is no shame between lovers. Nothing ever matters at all while you're doing it. The normal world seems so distant, so distant in fact, it almost ceases to exist.

He came back to my mouth and I kissed him, tasting myself, which he tasted too. I pushed him back and kissed his bare chest all the way down to the top of his jeans. He moaned and stared down at me, wanting me to take his cock in my mouth. He thrust his hips out a little until I unzipped his jeans and held his dick in my hands. I marveled at the size of it for a moment, wondering if it would hurt when he put it in because it was so big. I bent down and gave him a little of what he'd given me. He held onto my head for a while but then suddenly grabbed me up under the arms and pulled me away from it. It was as if what I was doing was too much to handle.

I grabbed onto his face and we kissed. We acted like the adults we were, like the animals we were always trying to hide. And we didn't just taste the freedom sex gives, we ate it.

We continued to kiss and gnaw at each other until he turned me around. Oh, boy. I knew what he was about to do and the very thought of him mounting me like that was almost too much to bear. Even so, I bent over the table and he stuck it in. *Ahh!* I unexpectedly felt very, very complete. It was such a nice feeling, too.

I climbed onto the table as he penetrated me more and more, ripping me open for the entire world to see. He was fucking me, fucking me trailer-park style, just like I'd wanted. Clay had fucked me like this until I got tired of him; we'd only reclaimed it once in awhile. But once I had it, I couldn't get enough.

He leaned forward and grabbed at my breasts. I squeezed one and rose up so he could kiss my neck. We changed positions and we fucked with me on top, with him on bottom. I was bouncing in his lap and I was starting to come, so I got up off of him and drug myself across his chest and stood over his face. He pulled me down and buried his face into me, licking and sucking and making me want to *come!* I was about to burst. This was going to be a big one.

I lay down and we made it like an old married couple—missionary style. But it was fabulous, so fabulous. I had what I was looking for, what I always wanted, and that was a big man to fuck me like there was no tomorrow. And he was fucking me like the man he was. And as I came, shooting sparks of blue and black, I wondered, *now what?*

Now I was totally fucked. Total blue fucking ruin. But then again...maybe not. As long as I kept my big mouth shut. But right now, I wanted some more of *that.*

"The skirt."
From *99 Martinis: Uncensored.*

The setup: Mark finds out what sex with a stranger in an elevator is all about.

I had a few buddies in the mailroom, and a few here and there on the various floors of the small publishing house where we worked. We'd nod at each other in the halls, complain about "the man" in the toilet and meet for a beer afterwards to forget about it all. Sometimes one of us would pick up some chick and fuck her then the next day someone had a story to tell to help make the time pass.

But right now, there was this ass right in front of me.

I'd never seen such an ass. The way it wiggled, just right. The way it was shaped, my dear God, the sheer roundness of it. It was astounding, this ass. It was being held captive in a little black skirt. The skirt didn't so much cover it as hug it, squeeze it, and shape it. The skirt gave it a home. *Damn.* I'd never seen such an ass. It was almost as if it spoke to me. It was almost as if I reached out and patted it, it would simply smile and say, "Thanks, I needed that."

The rest of the body wasn't too bad, either.

She, whoever she was, turned around and glanced at me. I averted my eyes, stared up at the ceiling and continued rolling the mail cart behind her. I didn't pretend to whistle.

I noticed she was slowing down, as the end of the corridor was nearing. She was headed to the elevator, but so what? So was I.

She got on, turned and held the door for me. I rolled my mail cart in behind her, not taking my eyes off her ass.

Her shoulder length blond hair smelled of mangos. Was it natural? Did the rug match the curtains? I've never been much for blondes. They're okay, I guess, but nothing is sexier than long, shimmering dark hair on a pillow.

But that ass...

She glanced back at me again. I decided, that, yes, she wanted it. Should we stop the elevator?

Then it happened very quickly. It was as if a magnetic force was taking over us and all I had to do was lean in for that first kiss. So, I leaned in and she leaned back, grabbing my head as I buried my face in her neck and began to lick and kiss. She moaned softly.

The elevator doors opened momentarily. We didn't pull apart. Good thing that whoever was waiting on that door had left.

The doors dinged shut again. We glanced at each other. She lifted one finger and pressed the big red *STOP* button. I had a feeling she was gonna do that all along. She turned to me and I turned to her. We stared without hesitancy at each other. We knew what we were gonna do. Here we were—strangers. Strangers who were about to get acquainted in the best kind of way.

And then we fucked. How else could I put it? There was no other way to describe it. We fucked. We went at it like old lovers, like animals, like we didn't have much time. Her short skirt was up over her hips and my hand between her legs, feeling her wet, swollen pussy. It felt so good between my fingers. I jerked her panties off and threw them over my shoulder. She gave a little gasp and looked into my eyes. I stared back. She grinned and I pushed one finger deep inside her until she moaned.

She grabbed the front of my jeans and began to stoke my dick, she began to rub it, fondle it, press herself up against it like it was the most important thing to her. And it jumped to life, becoming so rock hard it quivered. It wanted her so bad. It wanted her hands around it, giving it a good, hard stroke. I took her hand and helped her unzip my fly. Then she was down on her knees, giving me head. I held her head there, enjoying the way her wet lips kissed my shaft, then sucked on the tip. Damn, I could stay like this all day long. I stared down at her. She stared up at me with my dick in her mouth; her red lipstick was smeared slightly across it. She got back on task, sucking it so hard I could have come in a second flat.

I, then, realized we didn't have much time.

I pulled her up. She grabbed onto my face with her hands and we were suddenly on the floor of the elevator, her legs in the air, my dick inside her. I pounded against her as hard as I could. She wanted more. I gave her more, each stroke bringing us closer to the end of our ride.

She moaned and arched away from the floor. I pushed my hand inside her shirt and squeezed her breast, pinching at her nipple and waited. She moaned louder and louder and

I knew she was coming. A flood of good feeling wrapped around me as I realized I was giving her this, this experience, this orgasm, this time in space that only she and I would share, perfect strangers that we were. I loved knowing she'd later think about this and maybe blush. I knew she'd definitely smile. I knew I would. I loved knowing it was my turn to come, my turn to fuck her like she needed to be fucked. Like all women want to be fucked. Fucked like a slut, like the girl next door, like a whore. Like a woman. I loved knowing that as I fucked her, her orgasm would be intensified. That, maybe, it would last as long as mine did.

I began to hammer inside her, feeling it come, marching right up to the pinnacle and jumping off, leaving me to soar along with it. I shuddered when I came inside her. I could feel her pussy tighten over my dick and squeeze. I stared at her. She winked. I couldn't help but grin back and covered her mouth with mine, wishing we could do it all over again.

But, alas, it was over and when it's over, it's time to move along. We pulled apart and smiled at each other. I grabbed her head, pulled it back and kissed her, thrusting my tongue into her mouth. She held onto me and sucked on it, moaning as I kissed her, as she was being kissed.

Then she got off on the ground floor and disappeared into the busy lobby. We hadn't exchanged one single word. It was more than perfect.

My life was like that.

I went back up to my floor and finished my day. Then, it was going on quittin' time. Just as I was about to leave, I noticed a brown envelope I had delivered to Mr. Palm laying sideways on the cheap carpeted floor. I picked it up, tapped on his door and then tried to hand it to him.

"Not another query!" he shuddered. "Throw it out, Mark."

"Okay. Night."

"Night."

Without thought, I slipped it into my back pocket and forgot about it. I met Tim and Bern downstairs and we headed to the bar a few blocks over. I told them about my exploit on the elevator and they told me I was full of shit.

My life is like that.

We separated at 12:00pm and I took the train back to Queens.

"Nice to meet you, Albert."
From *99 Martinis: Uncensored*.

The setup: Mark has now read Kendra's novel, 99 Martinis: Uncensored, *and reflects back on a scene he found of utmost importance.*

I finished the book over the weekend. The whole story was about this chick, Vicky, and her search for love. She never finds it and when she does, she throws it away with both hands. The sex scenes were phenomenal. There was this one scene set in a men's toilet that I had to read at least ten times...

"...he led me into the toilet and before I knew what was happening, he had yanked my jeans down and his head was buried, literally buried, between my legs. His tongue didn't flick against me—the way some men give head—he sucked at it, like the way he liked his dick to be sucked. I loved that feeling. I ground up against his face and tugged at his hand until it rested on my breast and squeezed.

He stood, staring into my eyes, staring at me like I was a goddess because that's what I was to him, a goddess. I had his fate in the palm of my hand then. And I was going to use it to my advantage.

'You're beautiful,' he whispered.

I nodded, but I didn't need that line at a time like this. I didn't like bullshit.

'Just fuck me,' I told him.

He turned me around. I straddled the commode and placed my hands on the wall. I stared straight ahead and felt his hands on my ass, scooping the cheeks up with the palms of his hands and stroking them. I began to squirm, tensing with anticipation. I felt his hard cock fall on my ass and he moved it down, down until it found its place. He pushed it in. I gasped, nearly lost my balance and fell over. I straightened up and moaned. Ahhh! *I loved the way his cock just filled me, made me whole.*

He began to fuck me. Fuck me softly. At first. Then he drove it in harder and harder until he was thumping behind me, inside me. I moved my hand down and began to rub my clit. I stroked it, loving the feeling of euphoria it gave me when it was tended to. I moaned and wiggled against him until one of his hands found my breast. He stroked my nipple with the back of his finger and his cock stroked my pussy. My finger stroked my clit. All erogenous areas were covered. I loved all the stimulation. I also loved knowing we might get caught, that someone might come in and catch us. Catch us fucking. I wished they would. I wished that it would be a big man. A big, tall man. I wished he'd come in and stop when he saw what was going on. I wished he'd gasp, then his dick would get hard and he'd want me, too. He'd want to be the one fucking me from behind. I'd want him to shove this guy out of the way and take a turn. I'd want his big cock to fill me. Pressure me. Overcome me. Overtake me.

I began to gasp as the fantasy, combined with the reality, began to burgeon. It was too, too much. I couldn't handle it anymore. I couldn't handle it. I had to come. I had to scream, I had to get it all out. My fingernails dragged down the wall, taking bits of paint with them as he fucked the orgasm right out of my body.

'Fuck me!' I screamed. 'Fuck me harder!'

He did just that. His cock went so far up into me, it made the orgasm extend and amplify. He had hit bottom. I loved that he had hit bottom. It was hard to take it, though. I couldn't take it. I began to pound back against him, sucking all this power out of him and into me. I wanted him so much then. I wanted that strange man that hadn't materialized. I wanted everyone, everything. I wanted the world.

And then it was over. For both of us. He shuddered and erupted inside me. He fell on my back and hugged my middle for the longest time. I wished he'd move. The euphoria was over and it was time to leave, to disappear. To forget.

I jerked a little and he moved. I stood up straight, felt a little wobbly, then bent and picked up my jeans. My panties were nowhere in sight. I sighed and put the jeans on, wanting to get out of there.

'By the way,' he said and extended his hand. 'I'm Albert.'

I nodded, but didn't take his hand. 'Nice to meet you. Albert.'

'And you are?'

I stared at him and wondered why he was bothering with the formalities. It was over and time to move on. Surely, he had to know that.

I shrugged and made my way out of the bathroom. He called something after me, but I didn't pay attention. What did I need to know his name for anyway? What could I do with that?"

"Torture."
From *99 Martinis: Uncensored.*

The setup: Mark recalls another favorite excerpt from Kendra's book.

In Chapter 10 of *99 Martinis* the main character tortures a man by masturbating in front of him.

"I'd show him. I'd show Albert. I'd show him that he could do without me. The best way would be to piss him off. Then he'd leave. That would get rid of him. And I could go on with my life. Without having to bother with him.

I reclined back on his bed and opened my legs as wide as they would go. His eyes darted to my between my legs, to the wet stain in my panties. To me. He couldn't take his eyes off that stain. Off me.

I grinned, but I felt a little vulnerable, a little nervous. I'd masturbated thousands of times, but never in front of someone. They always joined in. But I liked what this was doing to him, how it was making him anxious. And how it made me feel superior, empowered.

He started at me, towards me. I held up one finger and halted him. He nearly stumbled over his feet. I rolled my eyes.

'What are you doing?' he asked.

'I think I'm going to play with myself,' I said and did just that. First I began to unbutton my shirt. And I took my time, too. I did it slowly.

He reached over and tried to help me. I slapped his hand away.

'Why not?' he asked.

'I can do it myself,' I said.

He nodded.

'Go sit in that chair over there,' I said and pointed.

He scampered over to the chair, sat down, then pulled it up next to the bed. I wanted to kick him away.

'Oh, my boobs are so sore,' I said, moaning and began to stroke them. 'I just don't know what I'm gonna do.'

He stared at my breasts with rapt attention.

I stared down at them, too. They were nice, one of my best assets. They were full and firm. I loved having my breasts played with. It was one of best parts of sex to me. I grabbed one and squeezed it.

He moaned.

I glanced over. He had his cock out! He was stroking it while watching me. Who did the little bastard think he was dealing with here?

'Put it up!' I yelled. 'Put it up now or I'll stop!'

'But, but—'

I sat up and started to button my shirt up.

'I'll stop,' he said and put it back in his pants.

'You do that again and I swear to God, I'll walk,' I warned him.

He nodded then motioned with his hand for me to continue.

I continued. I pulled my shirt back open and let it drop off my shoulders. I squeezed my breasts together and rubbed the nipples with my thumbs. I stared over at him, loving the way he couldn't take his eyes off me.

My hand made its way down my belly and to the waistband of my panties. Albert watched, barely breathing. I slipped my hand in and began to play with myself, stroking myself. I almost wished then that I wasn't trying to get rid of him so that I could command that he put his mouth on me. But I wanted rid of him.

My finger was now inside me. It was up inside of me. I moved it around until I found the spot, and then I stroked it. My juices began to flow then.

He made a move to touch me. I put one foot on his chest and pushed him back into the chair.

'You better stay there,' I told him. 'If you know what's good for you.'

He didn't say one word. He knew what was good for him. I almost laughed. He was now a quivering mass of nerves. He was twittering and jerking slightly at this new form of torture. As he watched me touch myself, get myself off. And the kicker was he couldn't do anything. He couldn't touch himself. He couldn't touch me. He was a bystander and that's all he was.

He better get used to it.

'Get my vibrator,' I commanded.

He leapt up and found it on the dresser. He brought it to me, holding it out like it was a crown *jewel. I grabbed it, turned it on and rubbed it up and down, up and down then I pulled my panties to the side and stuck it in. I arched away from the bed and towards heaven. There was nothing like this in the whole wide world. This was the best feeling. No drug, no adrenaline rush could ever compare to this feeling.*

I looked over at him, at his nervous face, his hands on his knees like a good boy. He wanted me. He wanted me so bad. If I could only want him. He was the first guy in a long line of guys who actually gave a shit about me. Who wanted me to be happy. Who wanted to help make me happy. He should have known better. I wasn't built like that, for happiness.

"OOOHHH,' I moaned and nearly rose off the bed as the vibrator began to fuck me, as I began to fuck the vibrator. 'YEEESSS!"

His mouth fell open.

I rode the vibrator like it was a hard cock, like it was the only cock in the world. I rode it until it made me burst, made me blow up. I jerked this way and that, taking the orgasm, claiming it and making it mine and only mine. I rode it until it ceased, then I rode it some more and got a little more out of it. I rode it until there was nothing left, until there was nothing else to do but fall back on the bed in exhaustion.

I eyed him. His dick was still in his pants. And it was hard. I'd love to sit on that thing right about now. I'd love to have it in me. But it wouldn't help matters at all. It didn't go along with my plans of getting rid of him.

"Why didn't you jump on me and fuck my brains out?' I asked.

His entire face took on a total look of disbelief, of shock. He couldn't believe what he'd just heard. He couldn't believe he'd let that opportunity pass him by.

'You said not to,' he muttered and dropped his head.

'I knew all along you weren't really a man," I told him and meant it. "But now I'm convinced you're a eunuch.'''

Truth be known, I wasn't in a much better situation.

"Infatuation realized."
From *99 Martinis: Uncensored.*

The setup: Mark and Kendra have now met and things are progressing just as he would have liked, even though he's so nervous he can barely sit still.

"Look, I know."

"You do?" I was stunned. It must have shown on my face.

She nodded. "Any girl knows when a guy has a crush on her. Y'all think we don't, but we do."

Oh, that. Phew. "How can you tell?" I asked, hoarsely then cleared my throat.

"The looks. The holding of the doors," she said and scooted to the edge of the bed. "The way you laugh at the silliest jokes, the way you overlook my bitchiness."

Oh.

She bent down and took off her boots, then rubbed her feet into the carpet. She liked doing that, it seemed. She glanced at me to see if I was paying attention and continued,

23

"The way you watch someone in an airport, thinking they don't see you or know who you are, then make yourself known just as another man asks them to dinner."

I looked away, then back at her. She smiled and stretched her arms over her head. My face burned with her words, her realization that I was gone and, really, she didn't have the slightest problem with it.

"Oh," was all I could think of to say.

She stood and walked over towards me. She kind of dropped one shoulder as she walked, cocked her head to the side. She kind of smiled through her blue eyes, kind of laughed, too.

"Is that all?" I asked to break the silence.

"The way you go along with whatever we say, even if it's just a load of horseshit, like tonight." She stopped in front of me.

"So, it was all horseshit?" I asked.

"Most of it."

My heart beat wildly in my chest. I trembled. I was so nervous. She took my hand and placed it over her heart.

"See? I'm nervous, too."

I nodded and she lifted her head towards mine. Our lips grazed, softly, then she puckered hers and I puckered mine, and we kissed. It was the sweetest kiss I had ever known, that kiss. I was smooth, yet urgent; it wanted to lead somewhere else. I wanted to take it.

She placed her hand over mine, which was resting on her chest and moved it to her breast and squeezed it. I grabbed her breast and she moaned, then pushed me back against the wall. I bit at her lips, sucked on her throat and squeezed her ass, which felt as good as it looked. I wanted to touch all of her right then, that instance. Now. Right now. I wanted to feel her, all of her. Every glorious inch. I wanted to be so close to her I could feel the blood rushing through her veins. I wanted to be inside her, letting her know how much I loved her. I wanted her to know that. I wanted to prove it to her.

She ground herself against me, twining her leg around mine. I walked her back to the bed and undressed her, she helped and soon she was completely naked.

I took a moment to gasp inwardly at her body, to admire it. Some worship was involved, too. She was built like a brick shithouse. Her body was tight, toned, and one hundred percent woman. It was curved and soft. Curves always drove me crazy. They are pure woman, curves. Her body felt so good beneath my hands and mouth. Her nipples were standing erect; I stared at them then back at her. She stared back at me, sucked on her bottom lip and pulled me to her. I kissed her; she kissed me back then pushed my head towards her breast. Which one first? I took Number 2.

Good choice. She moaned. I moved down.

I went down and breathed her in, smelling perfume and soap and her. She moaned and wriggled and I began to lick and kiss and suck gently. I began to kiss her there, just like I had kissed her mouth. She moved her hips this way and that, helping me to find the right spot. She moaned more and her hands were in my hair, pulling. I slid my hand back and forth across her, she was so wet she dripped, then I put it partially in. She nearly rose off the bed. She was tight as she ground against my hand and face. As she rocked and moaned, and held on tight. Then she trembled. And moaned. She pulled me up and I got in her, pushing all of my hard cock into her; it was such a nice place to be, like I had always been there, always should be there, that close to her. We sat up and she got in my lap and licked the corners of my mouth before she stuck her tongue in, then sucked on mine. I had to slow down. It was coming and it was coming hard. But so was she.

She moved her hips, pushed my mouth to her nipple and gasped, "Oh, yes! *Come on!*"

I pulled her back, forced her to be still and hugged her waist, and felt it let go, all of it, inside of her. Then I was a million light years away, inside of Kendra. I was alone. It was just me then and this feeling, which was her. This, oh so nice feeling that I had done well, that I had shook hands with fate then allowed whatever to happen, happen. All the scheming had paid off. It was worth everything, all the worry, all the money. I would have done double, done double every single day of my life to be this close to her... She was so close I felt like we were one person.

I kissed her again before she pulled away. I tried to hold onto her, wanted to keep her this close, knowing this was the first and only time it would be this good, this new. It would get better, but it would never be new again. Not this new. Not this fresh. Not this close.

"Come on," she said, pulling away. "I've got to pee."

"It was his way or no way."
From *Breaking the Girl.*

The setup: Kristine knows not to disobey Frank. That doesn't stop her from trying, though.

"Please," I said. "Just let me—"

"No," he hissed and pulled my hand away from between my legs. "Not yet."

"Please," I begged. "Please just let me touch it!"

"No," he mumbled, then, "No, Kristine, not until I say!"

That didn't stop me from trying.

The belt cracked against my ass. It drove a ferocious welt into my skin and burned like fire. I moaned.

"Please," I begged. "Please, please, *please*!"

"No."

It's always the same with us. Always the same with me. I always do this. I always beg to get it done and over with before the show has even really begun. I just can't wait. That's my problem—impatience.

"I can do it this once," I said, my voice rising to fever pitch. "Then I can do it again and—"

"Shh. Be quiet."

I stopped talking, begging, pleading. Plotting. I wasn't going to win him over. It was his way or no way. And I knew that. So it was his way.

He bent down in front of me, taking my head between his hands. I couldn't see him. My eyes were covered by a silk scarf, the one we used on special occasions, like a birthday or an anniversary. We celebrated at least once a week, regardless.

He rubbed my face and kissed me. My mouth opened and welcomed his tongue, sucked on it, loved its soft edges. My tongue drew circles on his, arousing a soft moan from his lips that came from deep down inside. I kissed him, hoping to soften him so he would allow me to touch myself and get the torture over and done with. But he knew what he was doing. He was withholding so the pleasure—the orgasm— would be doubled, tripled even. So it would be so intense I would shake and shiver and moan and groan and dance and sing. And beg for another.

I ground against the bed, moving my hips up and down. I was *this* close. This close and I needed to do it. Actually, my body just did it on its own; I just followed it and allowed it to search out the spot.

The belt came down hard again, halting me. A scream erupted from my lips. It was one of those I couldn't stop. I wailed until my throat was dry and my voice cracked. Another whack, another hoarse scream, this one less intense.

He put a gag in my mouth.

This time, I couldn't take it anymore. This time was different from the last. The last time had gone on half the night. The last time we tried this was yesterday. I couldn't wait like I had then. No. No. No! I had to have it now. *Give it to me!*

I couldn't utter a word and charm him into doing what I wanted. I couldn't bat my eyes and make him feel guilty. I was totally helpless, which was what he liked best.

Then he got behind me and I felt him glide his cock into me. Ahhh! YES! YES! The end was near. I was exhausted. But soon I'd be released. Freed. Unchained. And it'd be worth it, all of it.

As he began to fuck me, he said, "Tomorrow, we're going to try something different."I cocked my head to the side and listened, hanging on his every word.

"Tomorrow, I'm going to tie you up."

"Out of my element."
From *Breaking the Girl*.

The setup: Kristine goes over to Frank's house for dinner.

Five minutes before eight, his limo pulled up. Jackie gave me a wink and a smile just before I threw open the door and ran down the stairs. Actually, I didn't run. You don't run in five-inch heels. You walk. Slowly.

Tony, the chauffeur/bodyguard, had just opened the foyer door when I got to it. We stared at each other until I burst out laughing.

"I was just coming for you," he muttered.

I nodded. "I know. I guess I just got ahead of myself."

He nodded and held the door open so I could pass in front of him. Then he raced to the car and opened the back door in a hurry. I smiled at him and got in. He shut the door and we were on our way.

Frank's house was located in the Garden District. Yeah, I had a feeling he lived there. He lived in a three story, Georgian-style mansion that was called the Chandler House. It was that old, old enough to have it's own name and big enough to dwarf the other mansions that sat beside it.

It was magnificent. I hated to admit it, but I was in awe. I never expected to be invited to one of these houses. And my poor, pitiful apartment that I had painstakingly cleaned and decorated with used furniture and flea market finds just looked like a rathole next to it. Before I saw his house, I'd actually thought I had a nice place.

I pretended to be unimpressed. I closed my slack jaw and told myself it wasn't *that* big. I'd seen bigger. And better.

The driver opened the door and I proceeded up the walk, up the steps, and to the door. I had just held out my finger to ring the bell when the butler suddenly opened the door. I jerked back.

"Good evening, mademoiselle," he said with a French accent. "Monsieur awaits you."

So formal. I tried not to roll my eyes because he seemed like a nice old guy. I gave him a friendly smile and followed him into the study. I also tried not to gasp at the size of the "front hall" or at all the expensive artwork or antiques or at the size of the double grand staircase.

It was just all so *gigantic*.

I affected an air of detachment and followed the butler. Frank was in a massive wing chair in front of a huge stone fireplace. He jumped up when we came in. The butler bowed and exited the room backwards, shutting the door softly on his way out.

I could tell he was at once pleased at my appearance. And with the dress. I knew I looked good. He knew it too. I was glad to see *he* had noticed. If he hadn't, well, let's just say, *I* wouldn't have been pleased.

"Good to see you," he said, eyeing me, my ass in particular.

I gave him a grin. "Good to see you, too."

"I see you got the dress."

I turned around, then back. "Yeah. Thanks."

He nodded. "Oh, no problem. You look absolutely beautiful."

Absolutely beautiful. I almost blushed. Yeah. He'd just said that. Absolutely beautiful. It was the best compliment I'd ever received.

"Thank you," I said and smiled a little.

"Would you like a drink?"

"Sure," I said and sat down in the chair opposite his. "Whatever you're having."

He smiled slightly then went over to the bar, where he poured me a glass of champagne—Dom Perignon. I took it, sipped and smiled.

"Did you ever hear that story of Dom Perignon?" he asked and sat down in the other chair.

I shook my head. "No, what story?"

"He was a blind monk who was also a cellar master," he said. "One of the problems that French winemakers had back then was keeping their wine from going fizzy. Dom Perignon instead found a way to keep the bubbles intact."

I nodded.

"It was something to do with the cork and bottle," he said. "Anyway, after he tasted the champagne for the first time he called, 'Brothers, come quickly! I am drinking the stars!'"

"Huh," I muttered and sipped the champagne. "That's really interesting."

"Would you like another?" he asked. "You're almost finished."

I shook my head, feeling somewhat uncomfortable.

"Sure?" he asked.

"Yes, I'm sure."

God, I was so intimidated, I was rendered shy. I'd never been shy in all of my life. We didn't try to make any more conversation. We couldn't have conversed if our lives depended on it. My heart was beating so fast. Was his doing the same? He gave me an uncomfortable smile, then leaned over and lit my cigarette when I pulled one out of my tiny evening purse.

"Thanks," I muttered.

He smiled. I attempted to smile back. The room shook with silence. The only noise I could hear was the occasional jingle of the trolley outside. And that was far off.

The butler knocked on the door, opened it and announced, "Dinner is served."

Frank stood, walked over to me and held out his elbow. I almost cracked up. I didn't. I put my cigarette out, grabbed my purse and took his arm. I liked the way it felt, too, his arm. Strong. It felt strong. Stern. He had strong, stern arms.

We followed the butler into the massive dining room/hall/big fucking room. The table was about twenty feet long, lined with elegant chairs, some of which looked like they needed recovering.

I sat down to his right, instead of at the end of the long table, which I would have preferred. We didn't speak as we were served some kind of soup, which I did not like, then some kind of duck, which I picked at, then some fluffy, chocolate thing, which I devoured.

Once the plates were removed, Frank leaned back and pulled a cigar out of his jacket. He offered it to me. I shook my head and pulled my cigarettes out. He leaned over and lit my cigarette, then his cigar, which he twirled in his fingers until it was red on the end and smoked like a chimney.

We smoked but still didn't talk. I couldn't take it anymore. I looked around the room, racking my brain trying to come up with something to say then I stared at the chairs.

"Why don't you recover these chairs?" I asked. "They'd look really good recovered."

He had been sucking on the cigar when I said this. His eyebrows shot up. I could tell he got a kick out of my question and he tried to hide his laughter, like I amused him. Like what I had said was such a sweet, silly little thing.

"What's so funny?" I asked, somewhat stupefied.

He shook his head and explained, not really in a condescending way, "When you purchase antiques, you don't reupholster them. You leave them the way they are."

I glared at him. How was I supposed to know that?

"I was wondering if you would ask me that," he said in a manner that made me think he wanted to lean over and pinch my cheeks.

I blushed. I felt insulted, though I don't think he meant it as an insult. Suddenly, I wanted out of there so bad I could have jumped up and ran to the door. I couldn't take the tension anymore. It was eating me alive.

He took the cigar out of his mouth, then wiped the tip of his tongue with his fingers and flicked a piece of tobacco from them, like some actor. I rolled my eyes at his behavior.

Why was he putting on a show? Was he putting on a show? And what did he want? Was it just sex? Or a game, something to divert his attention from his lush, but apparently boring life. What was his deal?

And what was mine? I was impressed. I had no problem admitting that. But I knew he'd never give me anything. Nothing. I'd go with what I came, maybe without so much of my pride. Maybe I'd lose part of my heart, too. But I couldn't imagine loving this guy. No matter how good looking or rich he was. No matter. It didn't matter to me. I could take it or leave it.

So why was I still sitting here?

"It's getting late," I said, sighed and began to stand. "I should really be going."

He touched my arm, making me stop. I shivered at his touch. My heart picked up its pace, from steady to skipping, then thumping, pounding, until it swam in my head. I couldn't think straight. For a moment, all I could think about was his hand on my arm. And how it felt being there.

I moved away from him. Quickly.

"Why don't we sit in front of the fire? In the study? I had Pierre make a fire."

"That sounds very nice," I said. "But I'd rather not."

His eyes narrowed at me. I'd pissed him off. I didn't really care, though. I was tired. This had really turned out to be nothing more than a dud with him being the main dud of the evening. I didn't like the fancy food or the fancy cigar or the fancy house. I liked comfort, hamburgers, and soft chairs. I'd never, ever be able to get comfortable here, in this house. And I knew it.

Like I said, I was intimidated. I was out of my element. Maybe that was his whole reason in bringing me there. I didn't have the energy to speculate, though. I just didn't care. I told myself I didn't care.

"Please," he said. "Just for a moment or two?"

I really didn't want to. But his look implored me. It made me change my mind. After all, he had been nice tonight. Not really overly friendly or anything, but he had been nice. Which was more than I had expected.

"I guess," I muttered.

He rose from his chair, extended his arm. I didn't want to take it. I didn't want to touch him again. But it wouldn't be polite if I refused. I took it and we went into the study, where there was now a huge fire crackling and steaming in the fireplace. It did give the room a sort of rosy glow and made it less imposing. Not much, but some.

We sat side by side on the big leather sofa and stared vacantly at the fire. At least I did. I knew he was studying me, like he had studied me at the club and in his car.

I turned to him. "What are you doing?"

"Nothing," he said and rested his hand on the side of his face. "I'm just looking at you."

"No, that's not what I meant," I said. "Why did you invite me here?"

"I like your company."

"Bull," I said. "You haven't said two words to me all evening."

"I think I've said at least two," he said, his eyes twinkling. "Maybe even three."

I tried not to be charmed. "I know what it's about, Frank."

"What?"

"This. I know why you wanted me to come here."

"You do?" he asked and seemed more than a little curious.

I nodded. "It's about sex, isn't it?"

His eyebrows rose. "Uh, no, I don't—"

I scooted closer to him. "Listen, I know you want me. It's okay, a lot of guys do. But I don't need pretension."

"I'm not pretentious. This is just the way I am."

I thought about the Dom Perignon story. Wasn't that a little pretentious? I stared at him, realizing he wasn't pretentious. He was just trying to impress me. It didn't make me feel any more comfortable, but it did make me see him a little differently. It gave him a sense of humility, of humanity. Knowing this about him gave me courage to ask something. Even though it embarrassed me to death, I was going to ask. So, I did, "Why do you want to sleep with me so bad?"

He eyes darted up, then down. "Who says I do?"

"Oh come on," I said, moving even closer to him, so close I could feel the warmth from his body. "You've had a hard-on for me since the minute you laid eyes on me."

"I don't have a hard-on right now."

"Really?" I said and eyed his crotch. He was right. There was no tent in his pants. "Just tell me why."

"You're very independent, aren't you, Kristine?"

"What?"

He moved closer to me. "You like being a stripper because you think it makes you superior to men. Am I right?"

I thought about it. I did take his assumption into consideration. But he was full of shit. I liked being a stripper because I liked the money.

"No, you're not right," I said and moved away from him. "Besides, we've already had this discussion once before."

"I know that."

"So give it up."

"Like I said before, you love having guys want you."

I didn't answer him.

He took my arm. I tried to jerk away, but he held tight and wouldn't let it go. "You like having all the power don't you, Kristine?"

"Don't call me that," I said. "No one calls me that."

"They should," he said. "It's a lovely name."

"Let me go."

I elbowed him. I suddenly wanted out of there more than before. If I didn't get out, there would be no going back. I knew that. I struggled against him, pushing him away, but he wouldn't let me go. I began to feel a slight panic sweep over me. This was going somewhere and it made me very, very nervous. All the same, I couldn't stop it.

He pulled me back down and we began to wrestle for a moment until I grabbed his crotch.

"Like that?" I hissed. "You're right. I love having guys by the balls."

I gave him a slight squeeze, just enough to get his attention so he'd know I could do more. He didn't flinch, only reached over and grabbed me by the hair of the head and pulled me back. I winced in pain. It hurt so bad tears sprang into my eyes.

"Ow!" I yelled. "Let me go!"

"That's what you like, isn't it?" he whispered hotly in my ear. I could feel his saliva.

I pushed him away and wiped my ear.

He pulled me back. "The only man that you're interested in is one that treats you like shit, isn't it? The one who can dominate you?"

I didn't know. I'd never really had a man try to dominate me before. They, all five of my ex-boyfriends and the one ex-husband included, had been like putty in my hands. I could manipulate them in any way I chose. And they had bored me to tears. That's why I was single. Why I hadn't just settled down with one of them and lived my life like a normal person. They had been too easy. Too easy to get, to have, to contain. I'd tempt them sometimes, yell at them, scream, do anything just so they would flare up. Just to test them. Every once in a while, I'd get what I wanted. Once I got a black eye. But he had cried like a baby after he gave it to me and told me he would have rather have cut off his hands than hurt me, even offered to do it. I had run away from him, using the black eye as an excuse for escape.

From what I hear, he still has his hands.

Frank stared me dead in the eye. I stared back and waited for him to do something. We stayed like that for what seemed like a long time. Our chests pressed close, our hearts beating wildly in sync. We waited until one of us made a move. We waited on each other to make the first move. I decided to go ahead and do it, since I didn't want to be there all night.

This time, I twisted his balls. He let out a wail and released me.

"You bitch," he hissed and pushed me away from him hard.

I fell to the floor. I stared up at him just as my emotions began to run wild. I went from embarrassment to shock to anger to loathing.

"Fuck you," I said, getting up from the floor. I felt a lump rise in my throat. I was almost in tears. I was also very angry, mostly because I realized that he did have me all figured out. To a certain extent.

He eyed me dispassionately. I hated that look on his face. I hated that I didn't have him figured out as he had me.

"Fuck you," I spat and felt the tears puddle in my eyes and fall on my face. "Fuck you! Fuck you! *FUCK YOU!*"

His look changed. He almost grinned at me. He loved my anger, my seething passion. He knew I was just a touch or two away from ignition.

"Yeah, come on, then, fuck me," he said and eyed me. "Come on."

"Right!" I scoffed. "Don't you ever touch me again, motherfucker!"

He looked up at me. "Your pussy tells on you, Kristine. It's all wet, wanting this motherfucker in there fucking you."

He reached out for me. Before I knew what he was doing, his hand was up my dress. I didn't have any panties on. You don't wear panties with a dress like this. I wish I had. I wish I had because his hand was between my legs and there was nothing there to stop him. He was fingering me and he was right. I told on myself. I was wet for him. For him. In this moment. Here. I was wet and I wanted him more than anything.

He knew it. I knew it. It didn't stop me from hating myself for an instant, then reverting back to hating him.

He didn't say a word as he stroked me. As he fingered my clit, the lips of my pussy, which swelled and yearned for him to do more. But he didn't. He sat a foot away from me with his hand up my dress and finger-fucked me. Finger-fucked me until I was dissolving into a mass of quivering nerves. Until I moaned and pushed myself against his hand. His hand rested. It became still. I moved against it, feeling my own hands on my breasts, wanting his lips there more than anything. Wanting him. I fucked his hand which waited patiently for me to do as I wanted. And just as I was about to come, he pulled it away.

I gasped and opened my eyes. "You bastard."

He grinned at me. A real shit eating grin. I hated him.

"So tell me I was right," he said.

Before I could change my mind, I slapped him. I slapped him right across the face. He didn't move. He did raise one eyebrow. But that's all he did.

I shoved him away and headed to the door. I was so mad I could have spit. I did spit. Right on his Persian rug. I was almost ashamed after I did it, but I couldn't help myself.

He was suddenly on me, on my back, shoving me to the floor. He was on top of me, pulling at my dress, trying to get it off. I rolled over and kicked him right in the head. He fell back with a thump and a groan. I scrambled up and hobbled in my five-inch heels to the front door. I'd never wear these things out again! But before I could turn the knob, he was at me, pulling me down, holding me tight and not letting me move.

"Off!" I screamed as he turned me around.

"Tell me," he whispered.

"Tell you what!"

"Tell me how much you want me."

"Get off me!" I screamed and pushed at him.

"Come on, baby," he whispered, his hot breath on my ear. "Tell me how much you want me."

I stared at him.

"Come on. Tell me."

Tell me, tell me now. Tell me how low I can go. Beat me there. Hold me down. Fight with me. Kiss me. Kiss me now. Bite me. Scratch me. Make me want you. Take me away. Don't ever leave. Do what you want to me. With me. Fuck me. Fuck me now. *Make me feel alive.*

He was waiting. I tried to turn away from him. I tried to turn it all off, all the emotions I had were running riot inside me then. I wanted him. I knew it. He knew it. There was no going back.

I was still breathing hard. He was still waiting. I breathed, "I want you."

"How much?"

"I don't know," I breathed. "I just want you so bad."

"You want me to fuck you?"

I nodded.

"Beg me."

I almost regained my senses. But I realized this was his game. This is what he wanted, what he got off on. I also realized I liked it, too. And I was willing to play along.

"Please fuck me," I begged.

"Really beg me."

"Please fuck me!"

"More."

"Please, please, please! Please, fuck me. Fuck me—"

I didn't have time to finish. He covered my lips with his. He was sucking the life right out of me, thrusting his hateful tongue deep into my mouth and down my throat. I pushed at him and struggled. I could barely breathe. But he kept kissing. He kept kissing, sucking, groaning, moaning. He was right. I was wet. I did want his cock in me. I didn't melt. I exploded. I panted with lust for him, grabbing his face and holding him tight so he couldn't get away.

I suddenly wondered where the butler was. I didn't wonder long. I was too into it to wonder about anything but having him on me, in me, fucking my brains out.

He was coming out of his clothes. I was coming out of mine. I don't even know how we got them off. But there they were, strewn all over the floor and he was kissing all of my naked body, which arched under his rough and desperate touch. He pawed at me like an animal, biting at my skin until I was covered with tiny red marks. His head went between my legs and he sucked my cunt, sucked the juices right out of it and into his mouth. I gasped and rode his head, fucked his head until I screamed with orgasm. Until I screamed with liberation.

Then he was in me, fucking me. His cock went right up into me like it had always been there and he was simply returning it. I gasped with satisfaction. I gasped for him. For the moment. For the fucking. And he was fucking me then. Fucking me like no other man had ever fucked me. He was fucking another orgasm right out of my body. I held on tight and rode him as he rode me, taking it for everything it was worth and refusing to let it go until I was so spent I couldn't move.

He came then, shuddered, fell on top of me and didn't move for a long moment. He held onto me tight, like he was never going to move, never going to let me go. I found my arms holding him too, holding him like I loved him and never wanted to let him go. And I knew, I *knew*, I wasn't just a conquest fuck for him. There was something else there. I didn't know what it was, but that hadn't been a conquest fuck. It had been about us, me and him, fucking. He wasn't looking to add me to his list. And that made me just a tad apprehensive. What did he want with me?

He said, "I want you to move in."

"Something strange happened."
From *Breaking the Girl.*

The setup: After her fall, Kristine is up and about. However, she still has to contend with her sprained ankle.

I was up in about a week. My face was healing and it didn't look like it was going to scar. My body was still sore from the fall, but the painkillers made it all easier to deal with.

I knew I looked like shit. I refused to go out anywhere and asked Frank to give all the house staff a week or so off. I didn't want anyone to see me like this.

My sprained ankle hurt like hell. It took me forever to learn how to walk on the crutches. First you have to put them under your arms, hold the hurt foot up—or out, whichever you prefer—and balance. That's the easy part. Then you have to maneuver the crutches by lifting them up at the same time to propel your body forward. By the time I learned to get around on them, I could walk without their assistance.

But before that happened, something strange happened.

One day I thought I was home alone and was walking around on the crutches and by this time I was getting around on them pretty good. I was downstairs in the living room and decided to go into the kitchen and get some tea. I got up and made my way in there. But then I thought I'd also like a sandwich. I was reading a really good book and wanted to read while I ate. So, I turned around and went back into the living room, grabbed the book, shoved it under my arm, then went back out into the hall.

As I hobbled, the book fell out from under my arm.

"Shit," I said and bent over to pick it up. But I lost my balance and fell flat on my ass and my foot went behind and twisted. Again. The crutches fell noisily beside me.

I cried out in pain and started to cuss.

"Motherfucking shit!" I cried as tears began to stream down my face. It hurt like absolute hell. It was a sharp pain, way down deep in the bone. I felt it in my nerves, too. It was a taunting, deep pain.

I sat there for a few minutes and cried like a baby. And that's what I felt like, a baby who needed its rest and food and sleep. I needed someone to help me then, to help me up, to give me a painkiller. I just needed someone because I couldn't move.

I suddenly got the feeling that I wasn't alone.

I looked up and my eyes were met directly with Frank's. He was staring at me, mesmerized. I stared back and wondered what he was doing. He didn't move. He was transfixed by something. I wanted to say something, to call out to him, but I was almost afraid to break the spell.

I didn't have to say anything. In a second flat, he sprinted over towards me. He bent to my eye level and stared into my eyes.

"Does it hurt much?" he asked softly, but with an intensity that was a little peculiar.

I shrugged and wiped my face off with the back of my hand. "Not always, but now it does. I twisted it again."

He stared at me. "I'm sorry, baby."

"I know, Frank, you tell me everyday."

"No, I mean I'm sorry it hurts."

I stared at him. What was he getting at? "Me, too," I said a little uneasily.

"Would you like me to rub it?" he asked. "Would that make it feel better?"

"Maybe," I said.

He sat down and motioned for me to give him my foot. I stretched my leg out, laid it in his lap and he took my foot between his hands and began to rub it, ever so gently.

"It's all swollen," he said.

I nodded. "Yup."

He continued to rub it, holding it in both hands. He rubbed it like a nurse would, carefully. But then he rubbed a little too hard.

I gasped and said, "Shit! Watch it!"

He stopped and stared at me. "I'm sorry. I didn't mean to do that."

I sighed and sat back. "It's okay. Just be careful."

He nodded quietly and began to rub then he stopped and stared at me. "Can I take your bandage off?"

"Why?"

"I dunno. I just want to see your ankle."

God, he's so weird, I thought, but nodded anyway. "Sure, go ahead, but be careful."

He grinned and took off the clasps, set them to the side, then began to unravel the bandage.

"You have to put it back on, though," I said as he unraveled the last of it.

"I will."

"I know you will."

He held my foot in his hands and stared at it. I stared, too. It was swollen and black and blue. It looked awful.

He bent and kissed it. I smiled. Then he pressed his face against it.

"What are you doing?" I asked.

He shrugged and smiled at me. "Nothing."

I chuckled. "You are doing something, Frank. Tell me."

"No," he said and began to lick my ankle, all over the sore spot. I sighed. Ahh, that felt so good.

"Like that?" he asked.

I bit my lip and nodded. "Yeah."

He began to caress it again. I began to feel it. I began to feel warm and want him. Just by his touch, which was so gentle and caring, I wanted him.

That was his indicator. He stopped rubbing and set my foot on the floor gently, parted my legs and bent over me. I arched and met his lips. He began to kiss me then, kiss me differently. It was a slow, amorous kiss. His mouth was open wide, then he'd shut it, like he was eating my mouth. I matched his kiss and did the same, which elicited a deep moan from him.

He pushed me back on the floor and tugged my shirt up, then dove between my legs, eating at my crotch through my shorts. I moaned and grabbed his head, tugging at him, letting him know he could take the rest of my clothes off. His hand unzipped my shorts and he pulled them down my legs, threw them over his shoulder and came back up the inside of my leg using his tongue.

By this time I was so wet, I slid around on the floor.

I grabbed at his zipper and pulled it down. He helped, pulled his dick out and put it in. Then he fucked me. I sighed with relief. For a while now, we'd been making love, which was great, but fucking was what I liked best. I liked the way his dick filled me then thrust into me.

"Ahh, yeah," I said and bit at his ear. "Fuck me, baby."

He did so and gave a thrust that made me pant. He took my leg and held it up, so he got in deeper. I liked that. I told him so. He grinned at me and kissed me again, then bent and bit at my nipple, which made me rise off the floor and meet him thrust for thrust.

"I'm gonna come," he moaned and buried his face in my neck, which he ate at like a vampire.

I held his head and grunted, "So am I."

And I was. I was coming fast and hard, being so turned on I couldn't contain myself. And it was a deep, intense one. So intense I grabbed out for him and scratched his chest.

"Ahh!" he yelled, obviously in pain.

"I'm sorry," I breathed but didn't stop.

He didn't stop, either. We couldn't have stopped no matter what. We were like two wild animals on the floor fucking like we were supposed to fuck and when we came, we both cried out in pain.

It was that powerful.

He fell away from me, panting. I laid there panting. We didn't move for a while. I noticed we were both sweating profusely. I leaned over and wiped his brow. Just as I was about to take my hand away, he grabbed it and put it around his dick. I complied and moved my hand up and down it, then bent and put it in my mouth. Even though it was rapidly deflating, it was still hard. And as I sucked, he came again, came right into my mouth, his sperm. Not a lot of it, but some.

He grabbed the back of my head and held onto it, held me there and he let out a loud cry as if it were the best thing he'd ever felt, but it hurt a little too.

I stared at him. He stared back. We couldn't believe he'd just done that. Neither one of us. He grinned sheepishly and opened his arms. I lay down on his chest and he kissed the top of my head.

"Do you just come again?" I asked.

He nodded and cleared his throat. "I guess maybe I didn't get it all out the first time."

"I've never seen anything like that."

"I've never done anything like that."

"Wow," I said and sighed. "You were horny, weren't you?"

"Yes, I was."

"Why were you so horny? We just had sex this morning."

"Why do you always ask these stupid questions? I'm always horny for you, you know that."

I grinned. I did know it, but it felt good to hear, too.

"Thanks for rubbing my ankle," I said, then laughed. "Why did you do that?"

He shrugged.

I sat up on my elbow and stared him down. "Tell me."

He said, "I don't know what came over me, but when I saw you like that, all weak and helpless, it just drove me crazy."

"Really?"

He nodded.

"Did it turn you on?"

"Yes, it did. Tremendously."

"Wow," was all I could think of to say. "What else turns you on?"

He smiled, but didn't reply. I was about to find out.

"A terrible cook."
From *Breaking the Girl.*

The setup: Frank and Kristine begin to play games, starting with supper...

After the sprained ankle incident, things began to change in our relationship. All relationships are about sex to a certain degree, but ours became about games. And that's what started the games. That's where the door cracked, then swung wide open.

It all started innocently enough. I guess it was just a natural progression in our relationship. They were fun games, silly even. They made us laugh. The day after a game was played, I'd sit and think about it and just crack up. They were that fun.

Just after I was done with the crutches, the phone rang about ten in the morning. It was a Wednesday.

"Hello?"

"Kristine," Frank said, calling from work, or whatever he called it.

"*Franklin.*"

"Kristine," he said. "I've given Pierre and cook the day off."

"Ohhh...kay."

"What are you going to do?"

"Going to do?" I asked and glanced around the living room. "Just watch some TV or..."

"No," he said, silencing me. "What are you going to do for supper?"

"Oh!" I exclaimed and thought about it. "I could order in or maybe we could—"

"No," he said, again silencing me. "You will not. You will cook supper for us tonight."

I wasn't so convinced. Cook? For him? There was no way. I made a mean spaghetti and meatballs, but he wasn't the spaghetti and meatballs kinda guy. He ate veal that had little green things sprinkled all over it. He ate things I couldn't pronounce. He ate things I didn't like to eat because I didn't like fancy food. I was too meat and potatoes for escargot or any of that other fancy crap. Besides, I wasn't going to eat snails even if they did give them a fancy crème sauce and a fancy name to go along with them. Nuh uh. No.

He cut into my thoughts, "I have prepared a menu."

"Tonight?" I asked hesitantly. "You want me to cook tonight?"

"Yes, Kristine," he said, losing patience. "You will cook for us tonight."

"I will?"

"Yes!"

I still wasn't convinced.

"Kristine," he said in that warning voice. "Listen to me. I have prepared a menu, which I will fax to the house."

"If you say so," I said and stifled a yawn.

"You will receive it shortly," he said and hung up.

I stared at the receiver then set the phone down. Not a minute later, the fax machine on the desk was spitting out a menu. I grabbed it. Menu: Pot roast, mashed potatoes, green beans, rolls, lime jello.

Lime jello?

Well, that was certainly an all-American meal. I smiled. I could do this in no time. He must have guessed I couldn't cook anything fancy.

I rushed to the grocery store, bought up the items, rushed back and found a crock-pot in the cabinet. I prepared the pot roast, stuck it in there and started peeling the potatoes. I worked my ass off until about two that afternoon, only stopping once to light a cigarette, which dangled from my lips as I chopped vegetables, like a short-order cook in a greasy spoon.

He called around four. "I will be home at six. I expect supper to be on the table."

Then I suddenly got it. He was acting like a man—a man with a woman at home, who stayed home, who cooked for him, who took care of him.

He continued, "I have purchased you a dress, which will arrive at the house shortly. Please put it on, with the stockings and the heels."

"Yes, sir," I teased.

He growled, "Don't 'yes, sir', me."

"Uh, sorry. Sir."

"Kristine," he said. "I am your husband. You don't have to call me sir."

My husband? Well, well, well. And I didn't even remember the wedding.

"Can I call you master then?" I teased, twirling the phone cord around my fingers. "Please, master."

"No," he said. "You can only refer to me tonight as 'honey'."

"'Honey'?"

"Yes. 'Honey'."

"Okay, honey."

The doorbell rang.

"Go get that," he ordered. "That will be your dress."

"Bye!" I squealed and hung up before he could respond. I ran to the door, threw it open and a tall, elegantly dressed woman jerked back.

"Oh, sorry," she drawled. "Are you Kristine?"

"Yes, that's me."

"I'm Liddy," she said and patted a thin dress box. "This is for you."

I reached out for it. She held it back.

"No, sweetie," she said, smiling as if she were embarrassed for me. "I have to make sure it fits."

"Oh," I said. "Okay."

I led her into the living room. She sat on the sofa and placed the box in her lap, like she was protecting it. She smiled. I smiled back and waited for her to let me have it.

"You'll need to try it on, of course," she said and laid the box on the couch, then opened it delicately.

I stood back and watched her, thinking she must have some prize in there. I was astounded when she pulled out a rather plain, but pretty dress. Kind of like the ones Mrs. Cleaver would have worn on *Leave it to Beaver*.

She held it up and smiled at me. "Please be careful. This is on loan."

I had to ask, "What is so great about this dress?"

She gasped. "It's vintage, sweetie!"

"Oh."

She nodded. "Your husband wanted it, but I couldn't part with it, so we worked something out so you could wear it tonight."

I didn't bother telling her Frank was not my husband. Or that that this was all a game. I nodded at her and held my hand out for the dress.

She shooed my hand away and stood. "Just undress and we'll make sure it fits."

Being a former stripper, I didn't mind this. The only thing that bothered me was a prominent bite mark on my ass that my "husband" had given me the previous night. But I had panties on, so I doubted she saw it.

After I was undressed, she held the dress out and I stepped into it. It fit like a glove, which meant I could barely breathe in it. It also smelled musty and the old cotton was rougher than any material I'd ever worn. But once I turned and looked in the mirror, I grinned. I looked like a hot fifties housewife.

She bent this way and that, tugging at the dress, then she sighed, "Well, you don't need any alterations. It fits perfectly."

I nodded and twirled around. "I love it!"

She smiled and touched my arm. "Please, be careful. This is a one of a kind and I have it displayed in my shop."

"Which shop?" I asked.

"Tree Jordan's," she said. "On Magazine."

I didn't know it, but I nodded like I did.

She reached back into the box and pulled out vintage heels, an apron and a set of pearls. Then silk stockings, a garter belt and a girdle. I'd never worn a girdle in my entire life.

"Now," she said. "With a little make-up and hair, you'll be the perfect housewife."

I stared at myself. "Yeah, I guess you're right."

"Well, that about does it," she said and tried to smile. I could tell she was having a hard time letting this dress go.

"I'll be extra careful with it," I promised.

"Please do," she mumbled, then let herself out.

"Poor thing," I muttered after I heard the front door close. I glanced at the clock. It was five. I barely had enough time to finish up the meal and to get some make-up on.

I rushed around and was seated in the "parlor" with a cigarette—in cigarette holder—when I heard Frank come in. I tensed with anticipation.

He walked in, ignored me, threw his briefcase down, and plopped in the chair opposite me.

"Hey," he muttered.

"Hey yourself," I said, unsure of where this was leading.

"Where's my drink?" he asked.

"Oh!" I said and jumped up. I smiled at him before racing over to the bar where I fixed him his favorite martini—vodka with an olive. I slowly walked back towards him, swinging my hips. I bent down, delivered the martini and stood back up.

"Thanks," he muttered. "What's for dinner? I'm starving."

"Pot roast," I said and sat down in his lap. "With mashed potatoes and—"

"Good," he said and pushed me out of his lap. "Let's eat."

I watched in befuddlement as he left the room and headed for the dining room. Well, alright then. I followed him. He was already seated when I walked in the dining room.

"Smells good," he mumbled then opened a newspaper and flicked it so the pages would smooth out.

I stared at him. He stared back, over the newspaper.

"Well?" he asked.

"Aren't you even going to say anything?"

"About what?"

"About anything!" I half-yelled, really getting into my role as the over-looked wife. "Look at this meal! At me!"

He eyed me, the meal. He nodded. "Good job, honey."

I stared at him. Well, he had told me I'd done a good job. I decided to go with it. "Thanks. Honey."

"Am I going to have to beg for it?" he asked.

I sighed loudly as if I were *this* close to telling him to fuck off then fixed him a plate, plopping the food down onto it. I shoved it under his newspaper, then sat down, crossed my arms and glared at him.

He didn't take notice. I almost smiled. He was really playing it up. He started to eat, while reading the paper, just like I wasn't even in the room.

He glanced over at me. "Aren't you going to eat?"

"Oh! Yeah, I almost forgot," I said and prepared myself a plate.

He shrugged and gobbled down everything on his plate. Then he looked around. "Where's my beer?"

"Your *beer?*"

He nodded. "Yeah. You know I like a beer with pot roast."

"Oh, sorry," I said. "I've had so much on my mind lately. I'll get it."

I hopped up and raced into the kitchen, where I located a six pack in the fridge. I grabbed one, then a glass and raced to the door. I stopped at the door, pushed it open with my hip, and sauntered in, really swinging my hips as I walked over to him. He didn't notice, so I stopped about half-way there and walked like I usually do.

He glanced up at me and winked.

I smiled and put the swing back into my hips and made my way over, stopping at the table. I bent over and poured the beer while he stared at me from the corner of his eye.

"There you go, honey," I said sweetly.

He nodded, sipped the beer, then he held out his plate to me.

"Yes?" I asked.

"May I have some more pot roast? Please?"

I grabbed the plate and loaded food onto it. I plopped it back down in front of him then I picked up my fork and moved my food around a little, staring at him from the corner of my eye.

He folded the newspaper, grabbed the plate, hunched over it and ate it like a truck driver. Or a coal miner. He didn't even pause to wipe his mouth. I watched him, mouth agape. Then he leaned back and gave a big burp. I cringed.

"Would you like some more?" I asked.

"No, thanks," he said, eying my plate. "Aren't you hungry?"

"No, I had a big lunch."

"Oh," he said. "Then you can clear the dishes."

"Of course."

"And bring me another beer."

"Sure, honey." I said began to clear the dishes.

"Be sure to wear latex gloves when you wash the dishes," he called as I carried them into the kitchen. "You don't want to ruin your manicure."

I stared down at my nails. He was right.

I smiled at him, kicked the door open with my foot, walked over to the sink and threw the dishes down. One of the plates broke in half. Shit! Oh, well. What did it matter? I went back in, gathered the remaining dishes and smiled at him. He didn't smile back. He now had his feet propped up on the table and was leaned back, smoking a cigarette and sipping his beer. I bent over in front of him to grab his plate and his hand came down and slapped me right across the ass. It stung like hell.

I jerked up and whirled around. "What the hell was that for?"

"An ass like that," he said, grinning. "Deserves a good slapping."

He slapped it again, this time squeezing it with his hand.

"Watch it," I said, going back into the kitchen. "Honey."

I washed the dishes in about ten minutes. Then I went back into the dining room. He was still in the same position, only his cigarette was extinguished. He eyed me.

"Honey," he said. "I want you to get up on the table now."

"Excuse me?"

"Get up on the table."

"For what?"

"I want to see what's under that dress."

I began to tense and tingle with anticipation. I did as I was told. I slid up on to the table and crossed my legs.

"No," he said. "On all fours."

I got up on all fours.

He grabbed my legs and pulled them apart and peered between them. I almost cracked up. What was he doing? Giving me an exam?

He sighed and I felt his warm breath on my legs. I felt myself getting warm, growing moist. He did that to me. He could just look at me and I'd be ready.

He laughed. "What the hell is that thing you're wearing?"

I stared back at him from over my shoulder. "It's a girdle. It completes the authentic look."

He shook his head, still eying the girdle. Then he reached between my legs and began to tug it off. I wriggled so he could get it down. He threw it over his shoulder.

"That's the ugliest thing I've ever seen," he muttered.

I laughed. It was ugly as hell.

His hand went up between my ass cheeks sideways, then down. He stopped to finger me. I was now dripping.

He slapped my ass again like I was a piece of meat. I wiggled and stared back at him. He didn't return my gaze. He just kept looking at my ass like it was the first time he'd seen it. Then he ran his hand up my leg, holding it, squeezing it.

"I like your stockings," he said. "And I see you have a garter belt on."

"Yes, honey."

"The dress is nice, too," he said. "Did you get it on sale?"

I smiled, playing along. "No. It was full price. Is that okay, honey? That I paid full price? We can afford it, can't we?"

He shrugged. "This time, but you're going to have to stop your damn spending."

I hid my smile and said very seriously, "I'll do better next time. I promise."

He was now fingering my clit, stroking it, bringing it and me under his control. I moaned and spread my legs wider.

"Honey," I moaned. "Climb up here and fuck me.

He only response was another hard slap to my ass, then a grunt, like he liked doing that, slapping my ass. I know I liked it. He squeezed it again.

"You're fucking the neighbor, aren't you?" he asked suddenly.

I tensed. "No."

"Don't lie to me," he growled. "I saw you."

"No, no," I said, playing along, pretending to be in a panic. "You didn't see me. I only fuck you."

"Don't lie to me, bitch," he said and I heard him pull his zipper down. "Is his cock as big as mine?"

He pushed it between my ass cheeks, running it up and down. It slid along happily, getting lost in my juice. I moaned.

"No," I murmured. "Your cock is much, much bigger."

"Then why are you fucking him?" he growled and pulled my head back. He began to lick and kiss my neck, suckle it.

"I just did," I moaned. "I don't know why!"

"Yes, you do," he said. "You did it because you're a little slut. Isn't that right?"

He gave another jerk to my head. I moaned with ecstasy.

"No!" I cried. "I did it cause you work all the time! You don't pay any attention to me! You don't love me!"

"Love you?" he hissed and let my head fall. "How could I love a woman who sticks another man's cock in her mouth?"

"I didn't do that with him," I moaned. "I only let him fuck me."

He leaned over and whispered, "Where did you let him fuck you?"

"Just up the ass," I whispered. "I told him my cunt belonged to you."

He laughed harshly. I knew he'd like that one.

"Come on, baby," I said. "Stick it in my pussy, your pussy, it belongs to you. I'd never let another man touch it."

He did as he was told. He stuck it in, filling me up with every single inch of his hard cock. He took me like a bitch. Fucked me like a bitch. I couldn't get enough. I wanted it all, then some more. More, more, more.

"Besides," I moaned. "You're fucking your secretary."

"So what?" he said. "She doesn't give me shit and she works cheap."

"She's a whore!" I screamed. "She sucks your cock every day before you come home! There's nothing left for me!"

"I got plenty for the both of you," he said and leaned over and kissed my neck, then bit at my ear. "Then some."

"But I want it all," I said and moaned. "It's mine. Your cock belongs to me."

"No, it doesn't," he said. "I can fuck any bitch I want with it."

He accented the last syllable with a hard thrust. I gasped. Then he grabbed the front of my dress, yanked it, and, consequently, tore it apart. It fell off me in pieces. I stared down at it. Oh fucking shit!

"Oh shit!" I yelled. "She'll kill me!"

He was fucking me, not missing a beat as he asked, "Who?"

"Liddy! The dress woman! She said this was on loan!"

Oh, God I'd never be able to fix it! I almost stopped him, but of course, I didn't. Forget the dress for now. There wasn't anything I could do. I'd worry about it after we were done.

"Fuck Liddy," he muttered.

Yeah, fuck her.

"Oh, honey," I moaned. "Fuck *me* harder. You like giving it to me, don't you?"

"Uh huh," he said and complied, driving his cock deep inside me. I pushed back against him, which pressed it in deeper and deeper.

He grabbed me by the hair of the head and pulled my face to his. He hissed, "I don't like it when you fuck around on me."

"I won't do it again," I said and begged, "Please, fuck me harder."

He gave another push. "You should pay for what you did."

"I won't do it again! I promise!"

"I think you need a spanking," he said.

"Noooo!" I wailed as he pulled out. "Don't!"

But he had me turned over and pulled off the table, and I was bent across his lap, my bare ass sticking in the air.

"I'm going to spank you now," he said and reared back. His hand landed on my bare ass with a resounding *WHACK!*

I screamed, "No!"

"I'll show you to fuck around on me," he said and gave me another whack, then another, and another until I was writhing in his lap, until I was squirming, coming, coming so hard I nearly fell to the floor. I wanted my hand—or his hand—on my pussy so bad then. I put mine there, but he pulled it back, held my arm tight and wouldn't let me touch myself.

"Please," I begged. "Please let me touch it!"

"No," he said and gave me another good whack, so hard this time I nearly jumped out of my skin and ran away.

"Please," I begged and tried to get my arm back. "Let me rub it a little."

"No."

Another whack.

"OH GOD!" I screamed. "PLEASE FUCK ME NOW!"

He grabbed me by the hair again and hissed, "Promise me you won't fuck him again."

"I won't fuck him again! I promise!"

He seemed pleased with my answer. I almost smiled gratefully at him.

He gave me one last whack, then bent and kissed my now red ass, picked me up, sat me on the table, then spread my legs and dove in, sucking and eating at my pussy, getting lost in there like I was lost in him. I grabbed him by the hair of the head and held him still as I wrapped my legs around his head and humped his face. Humped him until I came. I screamed as I came, screamed his name with all my might.

"Now fuck me," I said.

He got up, stuck it in and fucked me, pushing me back on the table, pushing me down and overcoming me with his cock. I grabbed onto his ass and pushed him deep inside and I didn't let go until I came again. Until he came. Until it was over. And when it was over, we fell away from each other gasping for air.

He glanced at me and said, "You're a good fuck, Kristine, but you can't cook for shit."

I didn't reply. He was right.

"Trust me."
From *Breaking the Girl*.

The setup: Kristine and Frank's relationship takes a turn in a different direction...

I sat on edge all day waiting for his call. It didn't come. He didn't come home until late and when he did, he ignored me, went up the stairs and into the bedroom. Without a single word.

I willed myself not to succumb to any anger. I willed myself up the stairs and into the bedroom.

He was in the bathroom, brushing his teeth. I went in, sat on the commode and stared straight ahead. He ignored me.

"Frank?" I said.

He didn't respond.

"Why are you mad at me?"

"You know why."

"I do?"

He shook his head. "Yes, you do. Now leave me alone."

He was right. Damn him. I had to give it all over to him to experience this intensity he wanted us to experience. I knew that. But I wasn't ready. I didn't know if I would ever be ready for it.

"Did you masturbate today?" he asked.

I jerked at his question then stared back at the wall, almost embarrassed. Well, yeah, I had. But I didn't tell him that. I lied, "No, I didn't."

He stared back at me, his head nodding slightly. "Bring me your toys."

"What?"

"You heard me."

"No," I said, crossing my arms, thinking of my vibrator. No way was I giving that up.

He sighed and went back to looking at himself in the mirror. He ran his hand over his face once. I sighed.

He said, "You masturbated today, didn't you?"

It wasn't so much a question as an accusation.

"Yeah," he said. "You did. I know you did."

How in the hell did he know that? It's like he could just tell, even after I'd lied to him. He must be psychic or something.

"How do you know this?" I asked.

"I can see it in your eyes," he said, all knowing. "I can see that you did it when I asked you not to."

I almost cried. I wasn't going to. I had tried not to masturbate, but then I started having this fantasy of us and the next thing I knew, I was on the bed giving it to myself, coming and coming quick. After it was over, I had another. And another until I was exhausted.

"How do you know?" I asked.

"I just do," he said. "I know you. You never listen to anything but what's between your legs."

I sighed. He was right. But why did that make him so mad? I decided to make it up to him. I went behind him and slid my hands up his back. He stiffened. But he didn't move.

I tiptoed and kissed the back of his neck, pushing my hands into his hair. Suddenly, he whirled around, grabbed my wrists and twisted me until I was nose to nose with him.

"I am not in the mood," he said, then moved away from me.

Tears sprang up in my eyes. I hated him then. I hated every cell in his body. I hated his blue eyes, his handsome face, his dark hair, his cologne.

I peered around the doorway and watched as he got into bed. I loved him. I loved every part of him, even this. No, no. Not loved. Wanted. I wanted every part of him. There was a difference. It was all lust now, the love wasn't there anymore. But it didn't make me want him any less. I knew he was holding out on me. Making me wait. Making me want it. Making me want it so bad I'd explode.

I went to the bed and sat down, not looking at him.

He eyed me and sighed as he said, "It's just that I want you to give more of yourself."

I was stunned slightly. *More* of myself? More of *me*? I was giving him everything I knew how to give and more than I'd ever given anyone else. I'd taken shit from him I would have never taken from any other man. I put up with it because I'd never felt this way about anyone else. He knew it. I knew it. It was no secret. I would pretend to love him, give to him until I was ready to leave. Then I'd turn it off. That was the plan.

"What are you talking about?" I asked.

"You hold back."

"I do not!" I said, indignantly.

"Yes," he said. "Yes, you do."

"How?"

"You always want that quick orgasm, instead of holding out for more. You're like a teenage boy."

My face flushed. Maybe he was right, to a certain extent, but wasn't that what sex was all about in the first place? Getting off? I wasn't into Tantric or any of that *Kama Sutra* stuff. I liked fucking and fucking liked me and we went well together. Why mess with a good thing?

"I don't know what you're talking about," I said and crossed my arms.

He pointed at my arms. "That's what I'm talking about."

I rolled my eyes.

"Yeah, go ahead and roll your eyes. You're very good at that, aren't you?"

"Fuck off," I said and started to rise.

He pushed me back down on the bed. I struggled against him for a moment, then he kissed me and I melted. Oh, yeah. Oh, baby. I opened my mouth just as he pulled away and he pulled quickly, abruptly, as if I disgusted him. As soon as I melted, he pulled away. And refused to let me pull him back down.

"That's what I'm talking about."

"What?!" I half-yelled, getting pissed off.

"Our games, these games, are fine," he said. "For beginners. We're not beginners anymore, are we?"

I studied him. I tried to figure him out, I really did. I couldn't. I just wasn't getting it.

He leaned and whispered in my ear, "I want to show you something. Stay here."

He jumped up and went into the closet. I sat on the bed and wondered what he was doing. I could hear him rummaging around. He came back a moment later carrying something behind his back, like it was a surprise. I eyed him, wondering what his hand held. Candy? A rose? Sometimes he brought me little gifts like that. Once I got a Cartier watch. Once a pair of diamond earrings. What was it this time? When he finally pulled it out, my jaw dropped to the floor.

He had a switch. Not a rose. Not candy. And most certainly not a watch. It was a switch, the kind pulled from a tree to swat the backs of children's legs when they're being brats. The kind my mother used on me from time to time to keep me in line. A switch.

He cracked it in front of me. I almost cracked up.

"May I?" he asked.

Before I could think of an answer, the switch came down and hit me smack dab on my outer thigh. I screamed with pain as it cut right through my skin and scorched the muscle. It hurt like hell. Like a papercut. That's what it felt like. Tears sprang up in my eyes, burning into them.

He bent down in front of me and whispered, barely audible, "Did you like how that felt?"

I began to shake my head. No. That would be a negative. It hurt too badly.

"Kristine," he said. "Tell me. Tell me now. Did you like how that felt?"

No. I didn't. I couldn't. How could I like that? He was inflicting pain on me. I didn't like pain.

"Tell me. Please?"

I didn't like it. I didn't like it. I didn't like it.

"Tell me."

What kind of sick person likes something like that?

"Tell me?"

If I liked it, then that would mean... What would that mean?

"Tell me."

Would it mean I was a sick person? That I had been brought to this level by him? What *did* it mean?

"Tell me."

No. No. NO NO NO NO NO!

"Remember the first time I beat you?"

Oh, yeah. How could I forget? I still had scars. Not from the belt, but from the fall, but scars nonetheless. Scars that reminded me of the incident, of his anger towards me. Of my fear.

"Remember how it hurt?"

Of course I remembered!

"Remember afterwards? Remember how I took care of you? Remember how it felt, especially afterwards."

I didn't like it. I didn't—

"You liked it, Kristine," he said. "I could tell you liked it. You liked having me in control of you, you being out of control, you liked it. A lot. Didn't you?"

No, I did not.

"You liked it so much you tested me," he said, his face in my hair, near my neck. I could feel his hot, sweet breath. He smelled like mint toothpaste. He smelled so good, fresh, clean. I wanted him so much.

"You've tried to get me that upset again," he murmured. "But it scared me. I was scared of it because I was afraid I'd lose control and really hurt you. But now I understand and I'm asking you. Did you like it? Did you like the way it felt to have no control? To not know how it was going to turn out? To give yourself over to that moment?"

That moment. Oh, God, that moment. That moment where nothing made sense but everything did. That moment where I was at my weakest, yet I'd never felt stronger. That moment where everything fell from the Earth and I could care less. That moment when clarity took over and suddenly I knew what it was all about, all of it. And everything was about that moment—every single thing. And I'd wanted it back so I could feel alive, so I could get that close to him again, that under his skin, that close. So close I couldn't breathe if he didn't tell me to.

I knew what he was talking about. And it scared me. I couldn't think. I couldn't think straight. I began to quiver, panic.

"The way you responded to me blew me away. And you've been testing me ever since, trying to make me do it again."

He was lying.

"You've been testing me ever since."

He was telling the truth.

"You accused me of sleeping with another woman so I would hit you. Didn't you?"

The other woman. Oh. Uh… Oh, no. Oh, no. It wasn't about that. It was about me leaving him, finding an excuse for escape so I could take off. That's what it had been about. But even as I sat there and tried to make myself believe it—and it was true to a certain extent—I knew he was right. He knew me too well. I could never admit it, though. I could never admit wanting to give myself over like that. That would make me as bad as the men who played these games, who inflicted the pain.

"Kristy," my mother would say. "Never trust a man because as soon as you do, they'll be gone. Out the damn door. Just like your damn daddy. And you'll be on your ass. Never, I repeat, never trust one enough to let them have control."

Never, never, never. Never let anyone have any control, have anything on you. They'll use you. They'll treat you like shit. You—

He said, "You liked me taking control and you liked me taking care of you afterwards."

Did I? If he said it and thought it and believed it to be true, than did I as well? Did I believe that?

66

"You have to know," he whispered, so softly. "You can trust me. Trust me, Kristine. Let's see how far we can go. I would never do anything to you that you couldn't handle."

I wanted to cry, throw up. This was too much, too, too much. I wanted to run away and forget it all. But I couldn't. I was cemented to him now. We both knew we'd already crossed that line and now we were dancing along it, twirling, nearly falling, regaining control and laughing about it.

"Trust me."

Trust. Trust, trust. Trust him.

"Just this once."

This once… Now. Today. This moment. Trust him now. Do it before it's too late. If I didn't accept, it would be over. And I didn't want it to be over. Not yet. I was still having too much fun for that. And I still hadn't robbed him blind like I'd intended after he had thrown me into the wine cellar. I hadn't done it yet because… I didn't know why.

Then he did it. He gained my trust. He said the one thing he needed to say to win me over.

He said, "We'll take it slow, at first."

I couldn't control myself. I wanted to jump on him, fuck him, and have him fuck me. I wanted to succumb to his every wish, to his every desire. To whatever he wanted.

I breathed, "I'll do it. Just this once."

He smiled. "Then let's do it."

I reached over and found the scarf, which was lying on the nightstand, and handed it to him as an offering. He eyed me.

"Are we going to do it right this time?"

I nodded feebly.

"I don't have much patience," he said. "If you're not committed to this, I will be very angry."

I nodded.

"You sure?"

"Yes."

He said, "Now you have to let me have control. You know that. If you do anything that pisses me off, you will be punished. Severely."

I stiffened. Did he just say that? *You will be punished. Severely.* What exactly did he mean by that? And what did "severely" entail?

I started, "Frank, what—"

"This is your first and your last warning," he said. "You either let me do it or we stop."

Let him do it. Stop. Let him do it. Stop. Surrender or stop. Stop or surrender? Which one?

"Okay," I muttered.

"You have to totally submit to me, Kristine, in order for this to work."

Totally submit. Submit. Submission. Let go. Concede. Acquiesce.

I took a deep breath and nodded, staring up at him.

"So are we set here?" he asked, in a very business-like tone.

"We're set."

"Good. I assume you're ready?"

"I'm ready."

He blindfolded me before pushing me back on the bed where he began to undress me. He took his time, loving having me under his control.

"Relax," he whispered.

I couldn't relax. I wanted to but at the same time, something kept me from it. A sense of fear. A sense of panic. My senses became alert, ready. Steady. I could hear everything that went on inside the room. His bare feet padding on the wood floor. The ticking of his alarm clock.

The vent pushing warm air into the room from above. The soft bed covers. The silk of the comforter.

He rolled me over onto my stomach.

I felt the tip of the switch tracing along my skin. Ever so gentle. It rode along me, forcing me to tremble with anticipation. Then, all of a sudden, it came down and came down hard. Right across my back. *Ouch!* It was the papercut feeling. I hated that. I shivered.

His lips were on the mark now, kissing it, his hands caressing it, fondling it, easing the pain away. Ah, that was better.

"Would you like another?" he asked softly.

I was so excited, I could barely breathe.

"Kristine?"

"Yes."

And the switch came down. This time across the back of my thighs. It almost tickled. Then the sensation eased. I felt relief, release. Surrender.

"Can you handle another?"

"No," I said sitting up. "Not just yet."

He got up, turned me over, bent and kissed the tip of my nose. I began to quiver.

"Lie back."

I lay back.

"No touching yourself, okay?" he said. "Promise?"

"Yes," I breathed. "I promise."

His hands were all over me, the palms sliding along my body, kneading me, bringing all of my senses out. My nipples hardened and wanted his lips. I moved to the side, towards his face, but he pushed me back down.

"I'm warning you."

"About what?" I moaned, teasing him.

"I told you."

"Told me what?" I asked and almost laughed at his seriousness.

All of a sudden, I was turned, flipped onto my stomach and I heard a crack and his belt—not the switch—came down across my ass. I let out a wail that shook the chandelier.

"Why did you do that?" I cried and felt the welt on my ass.

"You know why."

I stiffened and started to take the blindfold off.

"If you take it off," he said methodically. "We won't start this game again."

My hands dropped involuntarily. I couldn't take another day without sex. Even if that meant he was going to give me a few more lashes.

He turned me back over and his hands began to play along my body once more. I moaned. It was killing me to lie there and not do anything. I wanted his hands on me, but more importantly, I wanted my hands on him. I wanted to touch him, his skin. I wanted to pull him tight and hang on forever.

He opened my legs and got between them, positioning himself there. I could tell he was staring at me. This made my juices flow even more, to have him stare at me like that. I moved a little, trying to entice his lips to move in that direction, down there.

"Do you need another lash?" he said as I moved again.

I halted myself. "No."

"Good."

I balled my fists up and waited for him to continue.

His fingers began to play with me then, one went into my pussy, moved around a bit, then the other stroked my ass. The pleasure was so intense, I nearly cried out. I bit my

70

fist and tried to contain the cry. Something came out anyway. I think it was, "Please."

He sighed, got up, turned me over and gave me another lash. This time, it didn't hurt. Well, it did. But it was different. It was so different, like nothing I'd ever felt before. As the belt hit me, I felt a deep surge of power from it, as if it were giving me power. I shivered and began to shake. It took everything in my body to keep me from asking for another.

Then, as soon as it hit, it was gone and I felt light, almost airy.

He turned me back over.

This time, he dove in, eating at me, licking, almost chewing. I moaned. He kept at it. I was almost there, the orgasm was coming and it was coming hard and then...

He stopped. "You're doing it again."

The switch came out and he began to tap me with it, lightly at first, then with more intensity. Tap, tap, tap. It went all over my body, every square inch of my body became alive as the switch played with me, teased me, controlled me. It wasn't painful, not really, it was more of a tickling sensation, just this side of irritating. I laid there and allowed it, allowed it until I couldn't handle it anymore and I screamed for him to stop, but he didn't. I begged and pleaded and I promised myself I wouldn't want it again, that I couldn't take it. It was too much. No orgasm was worth this. But just before I broke, he turned me around and kissed me, sending me into a totally different realm.

"Get up on all fours."

Uh, what? No. You get back down there and finish what you started.

"Now."

I got up on all fours.

He pulled my legs apart and then he began to eat me from behind this time, licking every crevice. I was so wet his face just slid along. He sucked at my clit for a moment, then pulled back and fingered it gently. I moaned and before I knew what I was doing, my hand was on it and I was trying to get off.

He didn't give me a warning this time. The belt came down across my ass. I let out one scream, then my body began to shake and I rode the tide of euphoria out.

I collapsed on the bed and gasped, "I can't take it anymore. Please do it."

He grabbed me by the shoulders and kissed me, pushing his tongue into my mouth until I moaned. He pushed me back on the bed and fucked me so hard it knocked the breath right out of me. But I took it and wanted more and I began to come then, so hard. It was like nothing I'd ever felt. The orgasm seemed suspended in the air, holding on to me tight, never letting me go. I screamed with it and screamed until it fell away from my body.

He turned me over and put one of my legs up on his shoulder then he put his hard, throbbing cock in me. He began to ride me then and I laid there wanting to move but unable to do anything but pant.

He was now pumping into me. I could tell he was about to come. He fell on top of me, taking my arms and holding them above my head. I began to move with him. We stared into each others eyes as we fucked and we reached that plateau together, nearly fainting in our lust for each other, nearly blacking out as we came together.

As soon as it was over, we didn't say one word. We didn't have to. There was nothing to say.

After that, the blindfold became a regular. This continued for a while, the sex becoming so intense, so powerful that we could do nothing afterwards but gasp for air. A few times, he incorporated a gag into our sex, so I couldn't talk. I mean, so I couldn't beg.

It continued like this until he said those magical words, "Tomorrow I'm going to tie you up."

"What will be…"
From *The Other Woman: A Story of Ménage á Trois.*

The setup: Clark is about to realize his greatest fantasy.

I came to on the couch. The first thing I noticed was that my shoes were off. And the second was that Carrie was holding an ice pack to my nose, which throbbed with pain. And the third was that Veronica sat on my other side with a wet wash cloth, which she pressed to my forehead from time to time.

"Here he is!" Carrie squealed. "Oh, baby!"

She hugged my head to her chest. I couldn't breath. I fought against her until she released me.

"Are you okay, Clark?" Veronica asked "I swear, I didn't mean to hit you."

Sure she didn't.

"Are you okay?" she asked again.

"Just a little dizzy," I told her and tried to sit up.

She pushed me back. "Easy there. Is your nose broken?"

"You tell me."

She and Carrie sat back and stared at my nose. They glanced at each other and shrugged, then Carrie leaned in closer, so close I could feel her breath on my face. She smelled like wine and cigarettes.

"It's swollen," she said. "But not broken."

I felt it and winced. It hurt like a motherfucker.

"Here," Carrie said and pushed a glass of water in my face. "Drink."

I took a sip, and then pushed it away. I stared at them. They were being really nice, too nice if you ask me. And I was sick of it all. I mean, I wasn't going to get anywhere with these women. They knew what they were all about and kept me in the dark. And they also knew every move in the book to keep me hanging on like some dumbass. I was an amateur compared to them. I decided then and there to give it up. They could do what they wanted to do. I wasn't going to plead or grovel or do any of that other shit. And if they were in love and ran off together, so be it. I was tired of speculating.

I sighed and stood. "I think I'll just go to bed now."

"Oh, no," Carrie said and jumped up. "We have to eat."

"Not really hungry." I started off but she grabbed my hand and Veronica grabbed my other hand and forced me to stop walking.

"Let's eat," Carrie said.

Okay, I guess I could eat a little something.

I allowed them to lead me into the dining room. They sat me down and pulled up chairs on either side of me. That was odd. I watched as they prepared a plate of food and put it in front of me. Veronica poured me a beer and held it to my lips.

"It's good," she said and nodded.

I shrugged and took a sip and Carrie pushed a fork at my mouth. I opened my mouth and she slid the fork in, staring at the food until I took it off the fork and began to chew. Once I did, she smiled at me and kissed my cheek.

"Good?" she asked and nuzzled my neck.

"Very," I replied.

Veronica got up and put on some music. Beatles. *The White Album.* My favorite. How did she know that? Did she know that? Had she—

I stopped myself. I wasn't going there ever again. What would be would be. And that's all it would ever be. So be it.

Yeah.

"Good chicken with rice, oui?" Carrie said and smiled.

I took another bite. It *was* good.

They continued to feed me, each taking turns. They wiped my mouth for me and then they…they began to feel me up.

I was probably imagining it.

But their hands lingered on my knee and then they moved towards my crotch. Just before the hands got there, they stopped and giggled.

No. This just wasn't happening. It was just a dream and I would wake up with a hard-on. I would jerk off, shower, shave and then go to work. I would work all day, come home and maybe watch some TV.

Their hands were now on my arms. Veronica said something about my arms being so big and strong. I had only heard stuff like that in my dreams and on stupid TV shows, so I ignored her.

"He is a very good man," Carrie said. "So strong and sweet and good and kind…"

Bullshit. She never talked about me like that. Her kind words didn't get my hopes up. I just sat there and let whatever happened happen. And nothing was going to happen. It was either a dream or some big tease. More than likely a tease.

"Oh, you got a little chicken on your chin," Veronica said and leaned over and licked it off.

"I see that," Carrie said and licked the same spot that she had.

"Mmm…" Veronica said. "You taste good."

"Oh?" I said and tried to remain cool. I *had* to be cool about this. Especially since I didn't think anything was going to happen. That way I didn't end up looking like a big jackass. They would probably laugh at me. *You thought we were going to do what?* I could hear them now. My ego would be crushed. I would have to smile sheepishly and pray they never brought it up again.

"So good," Veronica said and slid her tongue down my throat. "If I was a vampire, I'd eat you alive."

Really?

"So would I," Carrie said and began to nibble at my neck. "Oh, baby, you do smell delicious."

My dick was so hard it hurt.

Their hands were all over me. They were caressing my chest and my neck and my back and my face. They ran their hands through my hair and kissed my cheek and my forehead and my…

Oh, good God. They were getting down on their knees.

Wake up! I had to wake up! But it was real. It was really happening. Even if I didn't believe it and couldn't comprehend the enormity of it, it *was* happening.

Oh, my God. It was happening!

I stared down at them and Veronica unzipped my pants. She and Carrie helped each other pull them off as they stared up at me. I couldn't move. I couldn't think. I couldn't do anything. But I most definitely was not going to get up and leave the room.

And then I was naked from the waist down. My dick throbbed. They stared at it and Veronica smiled with what I hoped was approval. She leaned over and took the whole thing in her mouth. She deep-throated me for a moment and then came back up, then went back down again. Then she offered it to Carrie who did the same. They began to lick and nibble on my dick, suck on it until I thought I was going to explode. They kept at it until I did, until I came. I shot white cum across the room. It landed on the wall with a *thump!* Their eyes grew wide and they stared after it then back at me. Then they burst into laughter.

"Clark," Veronica said, laughing. "I've never seen anything like that before."

Neither had I. I didn't even know I was capable of shooting across the room like that. Well, I guess you learn something new everyday.

Carrie smiled and said, "Let's go into the bedroom."

They helped each other up, grabbed hands and started out of the room. They were still dressed. Both were wearing short skirts and little white tops. And high heels.

This couldn't really be happening. Nevertheless, I jumped up and ran after them. I found them settling on the bed. They didn't hesitate and started kissing each other immediately. They were on their knees, holding onto each other by their waists. They went right to it, sucking and running their tongues along each other's mouths and sucking face and...

Oh, wow. I was hard again just like *that.*

They began to undress hurriedly as if they couldn't get out of their clothes quickly enough. As soon as they were naked, they fell back on the bed and their legs intertwined with each other's and their wet pussies touched. They began to rub against each other, scissoring their legs together. They kissed and ate at each other's breasts as their crotches rubbed against each other's and the moans started.

Carrie glanced over at me and said, "You coming to bed?"

Veronica smiled at me. I was in. I was in! I was in! I was in in in in in! *YESSSSSS!*

I jumped on the bed and they pushed me down and started kissing me all over. They licked and probed and touched every square inch of my body and took turns giving me head. Each had a different technique. Carrie nibbled, deep-throated and licked. Veronica liked to suck and I mean suck. She sucked hard. It was wonderful.

They did this for a little while until they pulled back and, with haste, each of them tried to climb on top of me— at the same time. They nearly pushed each other off the bed as they both tried to mount my throbbing cock. They stopped, laughed nervously and stared at each other.

"You go first," Carrie said to Veronica.

"Oh, no, you," Veronica said and smiled.

"No, you," Carrie said, smiling. "You go now."

"Sure?" Veronica asked and glanced at me.

I nodded quickly.

"Okay," Veronica said.

Oh, God. Here it was. I was going to fuck her! And Carrie was going to fuck me after I fucked her! And then I could fuck each of them again and then—

Veronica grinned and kissed me. She sucked on my tongue as Carrie kissed her breasts. I just laid there. She bit her bottom lip, rolled over onto her back and opened her legs.

I got between them.

I slid my cock into her tight (and it was oh, so tight) pussy and this wonderful feeling come over me. I had forgotten what a new woman felt like. She was totally new to me and that made it all the more exciting. What was more exciting was the fact that Carrie was now kissing her as I fucked her. Veronica pushed back at me as I fucked her and told me several times to do it, "Harder!"

I did my best. Sweat was dripping from my forehead. They were sweaty too. We were all so turned on and horny nothing could have stopped us from fucking.

As I was about to come, Veronica pushed me off her and she and Carrie grabbed my dick with their hands and finished me off, then they sucked me dry.

If I died at that very instant, I would have died a happy man.

As I waited to get hard again, they went at it. They moved all over that bed and grunted like animals in their lust. They kissed and licked and played with each other as if they couldn't get enough. I know I couldn't. I could have watched them all night. But then again, it's always more fun to play.

When I was hard again, Carrie climbed on top of me and rode me hard, grabbing onto the bedpost. Veronica kissed me as I fucked my wife and after I came that time, we took a shower together. They rubbed up against each other up and up against me. We ended up on the floor, me fucking Veronica doggie as she licked and ate Carrie's pussy.

We moved back to the bedroom. Veronica lay down on her stomach with her ass in the air and sucked my cock as Carrie ate her out from behind. She would pause from time to time, pull Carrie up and kiss her and then she would kiss me. I was just so turned on, I was in heaven.

This went on half the night. It was all hands and legs and asses and tits and pussies and in the middle of it all, one very hard cock. I was so proud of that, that it was *my* hard cock that was pleasing them to no end.

When I fell away exhausted again, they went at each other. I didn't ask any questions. I wasn't a fool. I just sat back and watched.

Carrie began to kiss Veronica's naked body. As she did so, she murmured to her in French. I made out some of the words, "delicious", "beautiful", and "sublime". They were others, many others, but my French wasn't that good.

I smiled because she sometimes did the same thing to me. It was different now because I could see how she looked when she did it to me. It really turned me on and before I knew what I was doing, I was between them again.

We were up late, so I slept through my alarm. When I finally awoke, they were sleeping peacefully next to me, curled in each other's arms. I stared at them, at these two beautiful women and I just had to pinch myself.

Yeah, it hurt. Which meant it had really happened.

"The luckiest man in the world."
From *The Other Woman: A Story of Ménage á Trois.*

The setup: Clark and Veronica argue. Then they make up.

They were cooking when I came home, huddled over the kitchen table poring over a recipe book. I stood in the doorway and watched them for over a minute before they even noticed I was in the room.

"We need some chili powder," Veronica said and went to the cabinet.

"Cumin, too," Carrie told her and pointed at the cabinet.

"Got it," she said and pulled the spices out. She turned, saw me and smiled. "Hey, good looking!"

Carrie looked up at me and said, "Hello, darling."

"Hello. Ummm…" I stared around cautiously.

"Hungry?" Carrie asked.

I went to the cupboard and got some crackers. "No, I'll just have a cracker, thanks."

They stared at me and shrugged, then went back to the book. I watched them. Veronica sighed, picked up a bottle of something green and took it to the pot.

I intercepted it and held it back. "What is this?" I sniffed it. "Oh, God, it's rank!"

She grabbed it out of my hand, narrowed her eyes and said, "It's jalapeno pepper. For the chili."

"Oh," I said. "But it's green."

She turned to Carrie and gave her a curious look.

"Those peppers are green and a little stinky," Carrie said.

Oh.

"Are you okay, Clark?" Veronica asked.

"Fine," I said. "Just had a long day."

They glanced at each other and back at me.

"I'll just be on the couch if you need me," I said and went into the living room, sat down and turned on the TV. I fell asleep almost immediately.

"Clark?"

I jerked awake. Veronica was sitting next to me.

"Oh, Veronica," I said and sat up.

"How was work?" she asked.

"Fine, I suppose."

"Look, I know you probably spoke with Arthur."

"What?"

"All we did was give him a warning," she said. "He was getting out of control."

I eyed her but decided to play dumb, which I was good at. "I have no idea what you re talking about."

"You don't?" she smiled. "Well, good."

She slapped my knee just as Carrie came in pulling on a jacket.

"Where are you going, Carrie?" I asked.

"To my mother's."

"Your mother lives in France."

She considered, then said, "Oui," and was out the door without another word.

Veronica turned to me and smiled. "It's just me and you tonight."

I cleared my throat. She winked and loosened my tie. I just sat there and let her. When she had it undone, she threw it over her shoulder.

"Would you like a scotch and water?" she asked sweetly.

I shrugged. Sure, why not?

I watched as she got up and sashayed over to the little bar. Her ass was so nice and I appreciated a nice ass. It almost made me forget what a disaster my life was becoming. And that she was the main cause of it.

A moment later, she bought the drink back, sat down and kissed my cheek. "I know we haven't really had a chance to get know each other—one on one—so we're going to spend some quality time together tonight. Alone."

My eyes widened, then I cleared my throat and looked away. She cupped my chin and brought my face to hers and kissed me, first nibbling at my lips before slipping her tongue into my mouth. It felt so good, so right, but then it didn't. I pushed her away and stood up.

She sighed like she was getting annoyed. "What's eating you now?"

"I can't do it," I said. "I can't cheat on my wife."

"We've done it before."

"But she was in the room!"

"And? She cheats on you all the time."

My mouth dropped. "She does?!"

She rolled her eyes and said, "What do you think we do all day while you're at work?"

"All day?"

She laughed a little and said, "Just kidding, not all day, anyway."

I shook myself. This was a little too much. It just felt like a trap of some kind.

"Why are you so bothered?" she asked.

"Because I wouldn't feel right sleeping with you without Carrie being here."

"She does it!"

"It's not the same thing." I lit a cigarette and puffed on it for a good minute. She just sat there and watched me. We didn't say anything but I could feel that this was headed somewhere.

She sighed, got up and took my cigarette and put it out. "It is the same thing, Clark. All couples hit their peak and need extra-curricular activities."

"Look, our sex life was fine before you came around."

"Maybe for you it was," she said knowingly.

"What does that mean?"

She shrugged and went back to the couch.

I stomped over to her and said as calmly as I could, "I want you to tell me what you meant."

"By what?"

"That couples hit their peaks and all that crap! Is Carrie cheating on me?"

"Clark, it was a joke," she said. "I meant Carrie and I have sex when you're not here. You need to clean the wax out of your ears."

I grunted.

"You've been acting weird lately," she said. "Tell me what's wrong."

She motioned for me to sit. I didn't. I began to pace in front of her. I finally organized my thoughts and said, "Don't you think this living arrangement is a bit...abnormal?"

"You just love that word. Abnormal." She sighed and shook her head. "You're already said it a gazillion times tonight."

We stared at each other. I looked away first.

She sighed and said, "Maybe to some it would be 'abnormal'. I'm bisexual, so is Carrie. And you're...well, a man."

That's all I was, too.

She rolled her eyes. "How long did you and Carrie know each other before you got married?"

"Not very long," I said.

"What do you mean by that?" she asked.

"Well, it wasn't planned."

"But you're still together, right?"

I swallowed hard and said, "I suppose."

"Then leave it at that."

"Is Carrie going to be upset about this?" I asked.

"Who do you think suggested it?"

I turned to her and said, "Who are you, Veronica?"

She stared into my eyes for a long moment and then cracked up. "Geez! What is this? *Unsolved Mysteries?* Come on, Clark!"

I didn't crack up like she wanted me to. I didn't even crack a smile. I was so tense I could have jumped out of my skin. And over what? I didn't really know anymore. I was more confused now then when this whole thing started. I was over analyzing, that's all, but I couldn't stop. I was having obsessive thoughts. This was something good, very, very good and I should be overjoyed about it. But I knew there was a catch. There had to be a catch. What was the catch?

"Come on," she said softly. "Tell me what's wrong."

I feigned indifference and said, "Nothing. I'm just a little tired from work and…"

She looked at me like she didn't believe me and touched my arm. I jerked it back. She gasped a little and turned away, a look of hurt on her face. Why had I done that?

"Listen," she said with just a trace of animosity, like she was holding it in. "It wasn't my idea to have a night alone with you. It was Carrie's, okay?"

I nodded.

"You know, Clark, for someone who has it so good, you sure do act stupid about it."

I knew that but for some reason I couldn't stop myself.

"And I don't want to spend a night with you anyway," she hissed and stood up. "I mean why the hell would I want that?"

I stared up at her. She glared back down and started out of the room. She stopped and turned around, her eyes blazing. I was almost scared. I had never seen her angry before. But that's what rejection does to women. It pisses them off. I shouldn't have rejected her.

"What do you think of me?" she snapped.

"Uh, well—"

"Don't fuck around with me," she hissed. "You think I'm some kind of home wrecker, don't you?"

"No, it's not that. It's—"

"That's what you think, I know it is. Well, let me tell you one thing, it was *your* wife who came on to me, okay? I had never even touched another woman before her. And it was *your* wife who invited me here to live with you."

"Veronica—"

"You're a son of a bitch," she said, simmering.

"It's just—"

"Zip it!" she hissed and held up one hand.

I stared at her. She was really pissed off. Though she was short, she looked ten feet tall right then. I stepped out of her way before she turned on me again.

"And let me tell you another thing, you cocksucker, no man in his right mind who was in your shoes right now would be whining about it. You've got a lot of nerve to come home acting all crazy!"

She was right. She was so right. I felt like shit then. Real shit. It wasn't her fault the people at work were giving me hell. It wasn't Carrie's either. And I was lucky. But with luck comes responsibility.

"I'm sorry," I said and walked over to her. "I really am."

I laid my hand on her arm. She jerked away and slapped me. Her eyes were brimming with fire. She was so pissed off she could have spit.

"Well," I said and rubbed my jaw.

"You deserve a lot worse," she said and started out of the room.

"Wait a minute!" I yelled and grabbed her arm again.

She turned and began to swat at me at me. Her arms were all over the place. I grabbed them and put them behind her back. She kept struggling and let out a stream of curses that would have made a sailor blush.

"Youcocksuckingsonofabitch!" she spat. "*GET OFF ME!*"

"Calm down and listen to me," I said and held her as still as I could. "I want—"

She got an arm free and popped me in the jaw. I almost saw stars. I shook my face and turned back to her. Her nostrils were flaring and she was seething and...

She looked so damned sexy.

I pushed myself onto her and forced my tongue into her mouth. She kept struggling but then gave in and began to kiss me back. She began to bite at me, ripping my shirt off my back and jerking my pants down. I ripped her shirt off and grabbed her breasts in both hands. I bent down and began to devour them, sucking on them until they were red. I sucked on her erect nipples until she cried out and grabbed me by the head and pulled me back to her mouth.

We kissed all the way to the couch and there she turned around. Ah, yes! She wanted it doggie.

She told me to, "Fuck me hard."

I ran my hands up and down her ass, then between her ass cheeks. She moaned and began to squirm. I grabbed onto her pants and pulled them off in one swift motion. I tore the panties from her body. She was now naked before me.

I bent down and began to eat at her. She moaned again and moved against my face, purring my name. I sucked on her pussy and then began to finger her. She was so wet my fingers slid right in. I moved them around and placed my finger on her clit. That made her really purr. I loved that sound coming out of her mouth. She began to rock against me, shoving it in and around my face, making it slide around until she gave another gasp and screamed, "OHYEAHHHHHhhhhhhhh!"

"Now I'm going to fuck you," I said and shoved my cock into her.

She gasped. "Oh, yeah, Clark, don't stop."

"Like that?" I asked.

"Yeah," she moaned.

I grabbed her by the hair and pulled her up to me. "Harder?"

"Harder!"

I rammed into her harder. She began to shake and shimmy and moan even louder.

"I could fuck you all night," I told her.

"Fuck me all night," she moaned. "But do it hard."

I gave her another good thrust and she bucked up against me. She was coming again and she was coming hard.

I had seen her do this before but this time it was different. She was the only woman in the room and I could fully concentrate on her, on her moving and sweating and looking so hot and sexy. I wanted to eat her up she looked so good.

I began to feel myself start to come. And it was a big one on the way. My whole body began to tense. I rammed into her, wanting it to last forever, knowing it couldn't but being glad it was her that was taking it and she was taking it all. She liked it hard. I liked giving it to her.

As I came, I gave her ass a good slap and that sent her over the edge. She was nearly trembling. I was trembling. There was nothing we could do about it but hold on and hope it lasted.

But it didn't. When it was over, I fell onto her back and held her tight and decided that no matter what happened I was going to tell the rest of the world to go to hell. This was where I always wanted to be. With her and with Carrie, knowing they were mine. Knowing I was the luckiest man in the world and I would just have to accept that responsibility.

"Come here."
From *Now She's Gone.*

The setup: Bruce and Sandy have been married for a while now. You wouldn't know it by they way they act.

"Come here," she said.

I glanced over at her. She was sitting in the middle of the bed, her clothes still intact. Her shoes on the floor.

"Bruce?" she called. "Come here."

I stood in the doorway and just stared at her. She was so beautiful. I still couldn't believe how lucky I was to have her. Her petite body was held up by strong muscles, especially in her legs. They were so strong looking, so curvy, so feminine they looked unreal, like doll legs. She hated her legs.

I walked over and bent at the waist, bent down towards her. Her lips met mine, brushed them, then she leaned back on her elbows and said, "You do it."

I complied and took my time undressing her. I always did. It was like I was unwrapping a present. Inside the clothes was my gift—her—her body, which she shared readily. Which she gave to me, to the world without hesitation. As long as I shared mine, she would share hers.

I wondered briefly if she shared it with anyone other than me. I forced the thought out of my mind and pulled her shirt over her head. I stared at her breasts. They were popping out of the top of her bra, heaving deliciously as her breathe began to quicken. I bent down and began to kiss the top of them, to lick them, to nibble on them until she moaned and pushed me down, towards the nipple. I pulled her bra down and sucked on it until she grabbed me by the head and pulled me back to her mouth. She kissed me as I tugged her skirt up over her hips and she tugged my pants down.

I stopped and stared into her eyes. She stared back, her eyes mockingly growing wide and giggled. "What is this? A staring contest?"

I laughed a little and looked away, then back at her. "No."

"Come on," she said. "We don't have much time."

"We've got all night," I said.

"Shh," she muttered and grabbed onto my dick. "Give it to me."

I let her play with it for a minute or two, enjoying the way she stroked it. She knew how to do it just right. Up and down gently at first, then harder, with more pressure until I was about to burst. I felt the first bit of pre-cum. She felt it too and smiled up at me. She knew me too damn well.

I pushed her back on the bed and opened her legs with my knee. She went with me and spread them out, then her hand was on her pussy and she parted the lips and played with herself as she looked back at me. She was so wet she glistened.

I couldn't stand it anymore.

I fell on top of her and shoved my dick into her, drawing in my breath. That first contact between her pussy and my dick was always the best; it always made me lose my breath. Right before I got all the way in, I could feel her, all of her. And she belonged to me.

I took my time sliding in, enjoying the way her pussy sucked my dick in, enjoying the way it felt. There was no better feeling.

She gave an abrupt thrust and finished the job, pushing me all the way in. She grinned at me. She knew I hated it when she did that.

She told me, "I said I don't have all night."

I didn't reply. I gave her another good thrust, so good that she gasped.

"Harder," she moaned.

I did it harder, really ramming it into her. We fucked for a few minutes staring into each other's eyes. Whenever we had sex, I couldn't look away from her. I don't know why, but I just couldn't.

"Do you want to fuck me doggie?" she whispered in my ear as she licked on it. "Huh?"

I stared at her. She was already wearing me out. I loved it when she did that.

"You know I do," I panted back.

"Then do it, big man," she said and eyed me as sweat began to bead on her forehead.

I pulled out as she got up on her hands and knees, her ass pointing at me. I took a moment to run my hands along it before I bent and began to devour it with my mouth. I pushed her legs open and went for her pussy, her wet pussy. She was always so wet, so ready. I sucked at it until she began to come. And I knew she was coming because she never held back. She grabbed onto the sheet and began to pant, the panting would turn into a long moan and the moan would turn into a scream which would build slowly in her throat as the orgasm built then would intensify as it deepened. It would come out in a roar, softly at first, then with more intensity, "…ooohhhHHHHHGOOOOOOODDD!"

I loved that sound more than anything in the world. I loved fucking her when she made it.

"Oh, God, Bruce, fuck me!"

I gave her pussy one last slow lick, then a suck, then a kiss, then I got up, stuck it in and gave it to her. She was still coming as I began to fuck her. Her orgasms were always so long, so powerful. I felt that mine paled in comparison.

I leaned over and put my hand on her clit so she could come again. She loved that. She told me so as she moved against it and held onto me for everything it was worth. Her pussy just clamped onto my dick and never let go.

"Harder!" she panted.

She was insatiable. She couldn't help herself. She began to buck up against me, fucking me so hard I couldn't hold myself back and I began to pound into her, unable to control myself or her, just allowing my body to do what it wanted and it wanted to fuck her, every inch of her.

"Come on, baby," she grunted. "Fuck me harder. I know you can do it."

But I couldn't. I couldn't hold on to it any longer. I was coming just as she came again. She pushed me off, grabbed my dick, and began to stroke it hard until I spewed all over her beautiful face. I loved for her to do that. She gave me an extra treat and took it in her mouth and finished me off, sucking me dry. When she was done, she swallowed hard and gave me a mischievous grin. I grinned back and she came to my mouth and kissed me, pulling me down on her as she wrapped her legs around my waist and held me tight, like she was never going to let me go.

We lay there for a few minutes until our hearts slowed down. I let out a good sigh. Now *that* was a good fuck. I had to be the luckiest man in the world. I *had* to be.

"Get my vibrator," she said.

"Why?" I asked and buried my face in her hair.

"I want to come again."

I got her vibrator.

"She couldn't get enough."
From *Now She's Gone*.

The setup: Bruce has found and is now reading all of Sandy's dairies, after she's left. This excerpt is among his favorites.

"He was so nervous. He just started shaking like a leaf. I was too, but I tried to stay calm because I could tell I was going to be in control and the one who would get things moving. I don't think he was capable of even making the first move. But he sure as hell wasn't going to miss his opportunity. I sure as hell wasn't going to let him.

92

Good thing, too. If he'd chickened out on me, I would have kicked his ass to the curb. I don't like wimpy men. I once met this guy at a bar and planned on taking him back to my place and having some wild monkey sex. But he said, 'I don't have sex on the first date.'

I was appalled that he had said something so stupid. I told him, 'We are not on a date, asshole and after you said that, I wouldn't fuck you anyway.' What a damned idiot. Who are these men who have these kinds of rules?! Did they get them off some stupid movie or something? Or in church?

Well, Bruce and I got back to my place and I offered him a beer. I didn't have anything else. He said he'd like one. I got us each one and we sat down on the couch and stared at the damn TV and I thought, Fuck this shit. I want to fuck him.

I turned to him and smiled. He smiled back nervously and kept his eyes glued to the TV. Mmmm... Whatever.

The thing about Bruce is that he's hotter than Wayne and that's saying something. He's so damned good looking but, like Wayne, he really doesn't have a clue he is, which makes him even cuter. And he's tall, about six-something. I don't really know how tall he is. I just look up at him cause I ain't got much choice. Because he's so big, he makes me feel so little and delicate. I just always feel so good when he's around. Like I'm a little doll or something. I love to sit in his lap and stare up at him."

I couldn't help but smile. Because she was so little and cute, she made me feel bigger and stronger.

"I scooted over to him, took the beer out of his hand and put it on the coffee table. He just sat there and let me. Not one word came out of his mouth. I wanted to seduce him. I wanted to have him under my control.

Though I was very nervous, I began to nibble at his ear. I was terrified I'd slobber or something and make him push me away in disgust. I really liked him and had even considering waiting until he made the first move. But he was more nervous than I was and that might have taken years. I didn't want to wait years. I don't have that kind of patience.

I wanted this man. And I wanted him bad.

After I had nibbled his ear, I moved to his throat and began to lick it. He just sat there. Smiling to myself, I began to suck on his neck. I think I gave him a hickey."

She did. It was huge, right under my ear. I couldn't get away with covering it up with a cravat, could I? No, I couldn't. All the guys at the office teased and tormented me relentlessly.

"What did you do?" they tormented. "Burn yourself with your curling iron?"

I took it good naturedly because, hell, she had given it to me and I was almost proud of it. It showed her passion. And her determination.

When she came by to see me one day, they fell over themselves, ogling at her.

They all asked, "Is that her?"

I said, "Keep your eyes to yourself."

"He sat there and I put my hand on his dick. He was so hard. I moved his face to mine and kissed him,

licking his lips until he started to kiss me back. What a sweet kiss that was. It was perfect.

I moaned. We kissed for minutes, sitting there on that couch. I loved to kiss him. His lips are so great, so red and fat. I loved to bite his bottom lip and pull it out a little with my teeth. He loved me to do that.

After we kissed for a little while, I got between his legs, like a stripper (I had plenty of practice) and began to move my body up and down his. I gave him one damn good lap dance and he just sat there with his hands on my hips and held me there. He began to run his hands up and down my back. He rested them on my breasts, cupping them, squeezing them. I loved the way that felt. His big hands on me like that. I moved down and begin to nibble at his dick through his pants. He got so excited then, he just unzipped his pants and pulled them down for me. He couldn't wait for a blowjob and I gave him a good one. I eased into it, nibbling down the shaft then back up again, then I put it in my mouth and sucked on it. He nearly rose up off the couch. I took it out and smiled up at him. He was so turned on he couldn't smile back. He couldn't do much but sit there.

But then he did an odd thing. He grabbed me up under my arms, threw me on the couch like some Neanderthal and began to tear off my clothes, like he couldn't get them off me quick enough.

I loved it.

He just took total fucking control of me. All I could do was lie there and pant and moan and arch my back and wrap my legs around his head and beg him to fuck me.

After he had devoured my entire body—fingers and toes included!—he put his big dick right between my legs and shoved it in. I gasped. Then he began to fuck me, again like some caveman. And he knew how to fuck. This guy knew when to stop and let me get some. He knew when to start again, when to hold back so he wouldn't come. He knew every move in the book.

It was unbelievable. No. Hold on. It was UN-FUCKING-BELIEVABLE! After we'd been fucking a good ten minutes (and we were all sweaty) he stopped and was very still. What was he doing?

He whispered, 'Now fuck me, baby. Fuck me.'

I had never had a guy do that and I wasn't sure what he meant.

'Squeeze it around my dick.'

I didn't know what the hell he was talking about. I stared at him and he whispered, 'Your pussy. Squeeze it around my dick.'

Mmm... Okay. I tried that. He moaned his gratitude.

'That's it,' he said. 'Grab it.'

I did just that. He again moaned his appreciation.

'Now you move,' he said. 'You move and fuck me.'

I moved and fucked him. I couldn't get enough. I squirmed under him, our hot and sweaty bodies sticking to each other's. I wriggled and gyrated and then... Oh. My. God. I felt this enormous orgasm erupt inside my body. It started slow and then grew and grew and grew until I grabbed onto him and screamed, 'Fuck me!' He did. And as he fucked me, my orgasm intensified and I held onto it for a good two minutes.

*That's when I knew he was my man. He was one
I wasn't going to let go. He didn't really have a choice
in the matter. He was mine.*

After we were done, I said, 'Let's do that again.'"

She did. She wore me out that first night. She couldn't
get enough. But I didn't complain or anything...

"Reason to suspect."
From *Now She's Gone.*

*The setup: Bruce is still reading from Sandy's diary.
Unfortunately, he is about to find out something he'd rather
not know.*

"But I never gave Bruce a reason to suspect. But
*sometimes I wanted him to know. Maybe I thought it
would jar him a little and make him realize I was
around and needed attention. And sex! I needed sex!*

*I remember once going downstairs into the
kitchen and he was standing over the table, poring
over some stupid blueprints.*

We didn't say a word to each other.

*I sighed, picked up my gym bag, my purse, my
keys and a grocery list. That's when he glanced up.*

'Where are you going?'

*I held out my hands with all the stuff in them.
'I've got a few things to do.'*

*He gave a slight nod. I rolled my eyes and started
to the back door.*

*He said, 'Remember, we've got that thing
tonight.'*

I turned and gave him a disbelieving look. Don't succumb to anger! Don't succumb to anger! FUCK IT!

'I know, shithead, I arranged it and that 'thing' happens to be our fucking anniversary which you fucking forgot last fucking year!'

He just stared at me.

I snapped, 'Do I know you?'

'Don't start.'

"Okay! Bye!'

And I slammed the door on my way out.

I cancelled our anniversary date and we didn't make up for three weeks.

So, I had to have something to focus on. I focused on Peter. I had him over one night and gave him a good striptease, just like I used to give Bruce before he turned into the invisible man.

I took him into Bruce's office while he was away on 'business'. I half-hoped he'd come home and catch us. I knew he wouldn't. He would have probably said, 'Uh, please don't mess anything up in there. I've got to work.'"

Bitch! How could she have brought him into our house?! I would have beaten the shit out of that guy if I had seen him in my house!

"Anyway, what I did was put on the Otis Redding song The Hucklebuck and I had it blaring. Bruce hated when I blared the stereo. 'You'll blow the speakers out!' He was always onto me to TURN IT DOWN! Which, of course, made me TURN IT UP!

He wasn't there, so fuck him.

I stood by the office chair and I began to dance around it, swinging my hips back and forth. Peter stood in the door and grinned at me. I winked back and I pushed the chair over to him. He got in it and I went over and began to dance around him, taking my clothes off slowly. I didn't have a chance to finish the song. He grabbed me, threw me on Bruce's desk and tore my clothes off.

'Hold on, I'm not finished,' I told him.

'I can't wait,' he breathed and began to kiss me.

I loved the way he kissed me, as if he couldn't get enough of me. After he had my clothes off and I was naked and squirming on top of the desk, he began to touch my body. He ran his hand between my legs and opened them up. I moaned. This was the part I liked best. He kneeled down and got between them and just looked at my pussy. It was so swollen and hot. I wanted him to touch it so bad.

He ran one finger down my slit, then into my hole, as if he were studying it before he could kiss it. I could feel his hot breath on it and that made me warmer.

'Come on,' I said and raised my hips up so that my pussy was right in his face.

He pushed my hips back down and shook his head. He kept staring at me and his fingers began to play with my clit, gently stoking it until it throbbed and burned.

'Oh, God, come on!" I moaned and raised my hips again.

He pushed them back down and smiled at me. 'You're so swollen and wet.'

I stared down at him and nodded.

He pressed his face between my legs and breathed me in. His tongue came out and began to stroke my clit. I began to tremble. I was going to come. He pulled back and ran his finger down my slit again, this time all the way back to my ass. One finger went in back there and the other stayed on my clit and stroked it for a moment until it went into my pussy and he began to stroke it, like he was beckoning me. He had found my spot.

I gasped and felt myself grow extremely hot. I was so hot down there, I burned.

He pressed his face against my pussy again and began to suck on it. I was going to die it felt so good. One finger in my ass and the other in my pussy and his mouth on my clit. It was too much. I squeezed my breast and moaned. I began to ride his face and he kept it up until I was nearly bouncing off the desk. I rose up and grabbed onto his head and humped his face, taking everything he had. His fingers and mouth kept working and worked that orgasm right out of me and it was a good one, a huge one. I screamed as I came. He didn't stop and I rode it out until I fell back on the desk and whimpered.

He came up to my mouth and I took his face and began to suck on his mouth, tasting myself. I licked at him and helped him put his hard cock in me. He rode me hard, so hard I couldn't keep up at first. It was like something took him over and he couldn't help himself and he couldn't stop. I know I couldn't. I wanted so much then. I wanted his hands and his fingers and his lips and his dick all at once.

'Come on, baby,' he whispered and licked on my ear. 'Give me another orgasm.'

I was near exhaustion but I could try. He held still and put one of my legs up on his shoulder and began to fuck me. Then he did it. He hit bottom. I felt his dick way down deep inside me, pounding so hard.

I nearly rose up off the desk and I began to squirm a little and moved against him, staring into his eyes. He had the most beautiful fuck face. I stared at him and sucked his cock into me and I fucked him. He grinned and nodded and before I could help it, I was coming again, this time it was harder, a down deep in my pussy orgasm that reverberated inside of me before it exploded.

I dug my nails into his ass and screamed, 'COME ON! FUCK ME HARD!'

He fucked me hard. This intensified the orgasm and I held onto it until he collapsed against me. I continued to come, feeling the aftershocks of it for a minute.

And I always refer to that as the 'All Time Best Peter Fuck Ever.' I can't look at Bruce's desk without thinking about it."

Sweat was dripping from my forehead. I was completely enraged. I began to shake. "God!"

I jumped up from the couch and paced. Calm down. Calm down. *CALM DOWN!*

I couldn't calm down. I yelled, "DAMN!"

Before I knew what I was doing, I had the journal torn in half and had started on the living room. I threw a lamp across the room. It went into the wall. I kicked an end table.

I stopped myself and took a breath before I could completely tear the room apart. I know I was a hypocrite and I know she only fucked him to get back at me, but it ate me up inside. I felt betrayed, infuriated. I knew I was going to lose it.

So, I left the house, got in my car and went to a bar. I picked up a woman and took her to a hotel and I fucked her, thinking of Sandy and when I was done, I went back home, taped the journal back together and started reading again.

"Don't move."
From *Eager to Please*.

The setup: Kara and Nate are doing what they do best.

"Shh," he said and put a finger to my lips. "I'll untie you now."

"Please hurry," I begged as the pain shot through my arms again.

"I said I would do it," he said and began to untie the ropes.

I immediately felt relief, though only slightly. It took a minute before he was done and I began to whimper with pain. I don't know why it hurt so badly today, but it did. It was excruciating pain, a burning pain. It hurt so bad I couldn't stand it. It was usually more fun.

"Shh," he murmured.

Even though it's my pet peeve to be shushed, I shushed. Even though I was in so much pain I could barely concentrate, I shushed. He could shush me because he was in control.

Once the ropes were off, a feeling of relief, like a rebirth, came over me. The constriction was too much to bear. I stared up at him, almost smiling, though he was the one who had tied me up.

"Now lie down," he said. "It's my turn."

His turn. His turn to do whatever he wanted. We had played my game, the tying of me to the bed game and before that we had played my spanking game. Now it was his turn.

His game was fucking. He did the fucking and I hung on for the ride. It was the best part of the night. The other games were merely a precursor. They got us both ready for the intensity of what was really important.

"Don't move," he said.

I stared up at him, knowing what he was going to do. My heart began to beat wildly in my chest. He set the fire in my soul. He made me come alive. He knew what was going through my mind and that was, *Here I am, take me, use me. Do whatever you like.* And he would. Submission was the name of the game and dominance was inevitable. It was our favorite game, the one we played over and over but never tired of.

As instructed, I didn't move. I just lay there and let him look at me. I was naked, completely and utterly naked and not just in the sense that my clothes were off. He saw me then, he saw every single part of me from the tips of my toes to the curve of my earlobe. He saw my soul, my heart. He liked what he saw. I could tell as his eyes glided over me and settled on my mouth, which longed for a kiss.

Another pain shot through my arms as the feeling began to return from being bound. A cry came out of my mouth before I could stop it and I began to shake my arms to get them awake. It was a terrible ache I felt. I had to get them better.

"I told you to be still," he said, his English accent coming out strong.

But I couldn't stop moving. The pain I had felt earlier was still there, though it was numbing. "I can't," I said and held out my arms. "They hurt."

He eyed me, sighed and sat down on the bed. He took my arms and began to massage them until the life came back. I moaned. That felt so good.

"Is that better?" he asked.

"Yes," I said. "Thank you."

He stared into my eyes, not blinking. "Then be still."

I was still.

He got up and went to the foot of the bed and continued to stare at me. He loved to stare at me, take all of my body in. Although it was natural to feel self-conscious when someone looks at you like that, when he did it, it gave me power. I wanted to show him what I had, from the top of my head to the bottom of my feet. I wanted him to *see* me. I couldn't stand it when he looked away.

He looked away.

"What did I do wrong?" I asked.

"Nothing," he said.

But there was something wrong, something amiss. I could feel it, I had felt it earlier. That's why it wasn't as fun as it had been. I had to asked, "What is it?" though I dreaded the answer.

He stared back at me and said, "Tomorrow you're going home."

My mouth dropped and before I knew it, tears were spilling out of my eyes. I began to cry so hard I could barely breathe. *No!* I didn't want to go home! I wanted to stay here, in this dilapidated, abandoned house forever. I wanted to stay with him.

"Shh," he said again.

I couldn't stop crying, not even for him. The thought of being away from him, even for a minute, was killing me. And I wouldn't see him after tomorrow. I didn't know much, but I knew that. He'd be gone forever.

"I said to *shh*," he told me.

I stared at him and bit my bottom lip. He stared back and shook his head slightly, as if he felt sorry for me.

"Please," I said. "I don't want to go home."

"But you have to," he said and climbed into bed.

I stared at him, at his big arms that held me tight, at his hands that made me squirm. I stared at his handsome face, at the laugh lines around his deep blue eyes that crinkled when I said something to amuse him, at the whiskers on his chin that tickled my legs when he kissed his way up. I stared at him and felt a connection so strong it made my heart sick.

He bent over me and said, "You knew this day would come."

"I won't go," I said.

"You have to, Kara."

I stopped crying. "No. I won't."

He smiled. He liked my defiance; it amused him to no end. He almost laughed but then he didn't. His mind was on other matters.

"Don't think about it right now," he said and leaned down for a kiss. I rose up on my elbows and met his lips, but then he pulled away, teasing me. I couldn't help but smile, even though I felt terrible inside. He leaned back down and pulled away again, teasing me, making me come to him. He did this until I grabbed his face and pulled his lips to mine. We began to kiss, kiss like we always kissed. A little forceful at first and then we would begin to eat at each other's mouths.

I moaned, "Oh, Nate, you taste so good."

He climbed on top of me, pushing my legs apart with his knee. I pressed against his leg, feeling the coarse outline of his jeans. His jeans felt cool and unyielding. I began to move against his leg, allowing myself to scrape along it. He began to grind into me. His cock was so hard I could feel it even though it was still inside his jeans. It pressed up against them and made a big outline. I wanted it. I rubbed it and kissed his neck, sucked it. He moaned and moved so I could kiss his chest, then down to his dick, which awaited my mouth. He was squirming for it. He wanted to take as much as I wanted to give.

He rolled off me and I climbed on top of him, straddled him began to move down towards his cock. But he grabbed my hips and pulled me back to him. I bent over him and he started by kissing my breasts, grabbing them with both hands and squeezing them. *Mmmm*...I wanted more. He nibbled at my nipple then sucked on it before he pushed me up until I was standing over him. He grabbed my hips and pulled my pussy down on his face and began to lick and suck it, finger it until I was humping his face and wanting his cock even more.

"Ahh," I moaned. "Oh, yeah, oh, baby... Let me do you."

I pulled his hard cock out of his jeans and went down on him. He gasped a little. *Ahh, yes.* I kissed the shaft then slid my tongue down along it until I came back up and deepthroated him. He moaned. I stopped for a minute and smiled up at him, loving the look on his face as I controlled of him. I went back to his dick and sucked it with everything I had.

I didn't have time to do any more. He suddenly moved me off him, turned me over and put me up on all fours. Then he was on my back, licking it, kissing it, reaching around to squeeze my breasts.

I couldn't take it anymore and demanded, "Put it in. Now."

He didn't need to be told twice. I moaned as he began to fuck me, fuck me hard. I pushed back against him, loving the way his dick filled me up and made me whole.

Then I felt the first slap of his hand on my ass. *Oh, God, yes!* I shivered and wanted another. He gave it to me then resumed his fevered pace. I couldn't keep up. I grabbed the bed for leverage. He was going for it. He was taking me, consuming me, using me. It was dirty and slightly vicious and was what sex was really all about when you got right down to it. It was about getting and taking what you wanted. And what you needed.

Just then he slowed and bent over my back, kissing it. I moaned and began to wriggle. I trembled with delight as he pawed at me before he went right back at it. He slowed again and his hand came around and rested on my clit. Without hesitation, I began to move against it, moved until I felt the orgasm. It began to tickle me so I paused and moved against his hand and then back against his cock. I shuddered. This was going to be an enormous orgasm. Before I could enjoy the moment before the release, I felt it. I felt it then, all of it, it was almost painful, but so deliciously painful it made me want it more. That's when I took it and began to come and come hard, so hard I was wailing. A strange sound came out of my throat and that was his cue to take over again.

I don't know how long it lasted. All I know was that we were going at it so hard the bed threatened to fall apart. But that didn't stop us, even if the pictures on the wall were shaking and the windowsills were rattling. Nothing mattered as we fucked. Nothing ever would.

He came just then, just after my orgasm began to fade and he grabbed onto my ass and pumped into me so hard I thought I would break in two. He pumped into me and moaned and…then… He was finished. We collapsed on the bed, with him on top and tried to catch our breath. We lay like that for a long moment, barely breathing. The intensity always winded us.

When we were finally back from euphoria, I rolled out from under him, draped a leg across his chest and kissed his cheek. He grabbed my hand, kissed it, and then kissed me.

"I love you, you know that, right?" he muttered.

I nodded. "I love you, too."

He eyed me. I stared back. Say it, say it, say it *say it!* Tell me we can make it work, that we can figure this thing out. Make it work; give me some hope that it can.

He turned away.

I almost started crying again but I didn't. I couldn't. I would figure this thing out. I would make it work. I don't know how, but I already had a plan working and nothing was going to keep me from him. He was mine and no one was going to take him away.

"Let's go to sleep," he said.

"Uh, Nate—"

"Shh," he said and nuzzled my neck. "Let's sleep, love. We can talk in the morning."

"But—"

"Shh," he murmured and closed his eyes.

I thought about my plan. I knew what I was going to do. I turned over and we spooned. He fell asleep but I stayed awake for a while. As I listened to his breathing, I figured and formulated. I stayed up half the night and didn't move an inch from his arms. I wouldn't have moved for anything. I lay there and felt so sheltered and so secure and so wanted. I loved that feeling, of being wanted by someone who wanted me as much as I wanted him. It was a good feeling.

I tried not to fall asleep but before I knew it, I had. When I awoke he was gone. At first I thought he might have just gone downstairs for breakfast. Sometimes he did that and would carry a tray back up for me. He was considerate and wouldn't disturb me when I slept. He would let me sleep then he would bring the tray up, set it on the nightstand quietly and lie beside me. He would hold me until I woke and turned over to him. A smile would flicker in his eyes before it crossed his lips. He would always say, "How late can you sleep? It's nearly noon."

I stared at the clock on the wall. It wasn't even nine. And that's when I knew he was gone. I felt sick, so sick I could have thrown up. He was gone. He was really gone. And he had taken my heart with him. There was no way to get it back.

I jumped up off the bed and looked around. I don't know why I looked because I knew deep down that he wasn't there and that he'd been gone for some time. There was no "goodbye" note on my pillow. His side of the bed was cold. There was nothing left of us. I began to cry. I was crying so hard I couldn't breathe. I fell down on the bed and buried my face in his pillow, which still smelled of him. I breathed the smell in and knew that in a matter of hours it would be totally gone from the room and from my memory.

"Good God, Kara."

I froze.

"Put your clothes on."

A dress came flying at me and landed on my back. I turned and looked up. It was Grant, my husband. He was standing in the door dressed, as usual, in a business suit. He never wore jeans and he never got his hands dirty. He never did anything he didn't want to. I had never wanted to see him again. I didn't usually get what I wanted.

"We're going home," he said. "Now get ready."

And with that, he turned and left the room. It was true. Nate was gone for good. And I was all alone—again.

"No one else would do."
From *Eager to Please.*

The setup: Kara likes to test the limits with Nate.

Later on, I was in the billiards room playing pool by myself when Nate came in. It was the most fun I had since I'd been there. Besides doing the sex thing, that is.

He came into the room and didn't speak. Neither did I and we pretended to ignore one another for the longest time. I kept playing pool. He looked around and the look came onto his face. The look of anger and sheer annoyance. There was frustration there too.

"What happened?" he asked, looking around the room, then back at me.

"Eight-ball, corner pocket," I said and hit it, sending it on its way. I had won the game. Of course, the competition was weak.

"Kara?" he said. "What happened?"

"Don't know what you mean," I said and threw the pool cue on the table.

"You know bloody well what I—"

Before he could finish, I turned on my heel and left the room. I went into the kitchen and made myself another sandwich. He didn't come in there for a long time but I could tell he was dying to.

I was almost finished eating when he came into the kitchen. I hid my smile and didn't say a word as he stared at me, arms crossed. The room shook with silence and the faint ticking of the clock on the wall.

Finally he said, "This isn't working."

"You're right," I said and leaned back in the chair. "It's time you realized that."

His nostrils flared. "Don't fuck around with me. You don't know who you're dealing with."

"No," I said. "*You* don't who you're dealing with. You might have kidnapped me but that doesn't mean I'm your slave."

He didn't like that, I could just tell. He probably thought that fucking me last night would pacify me and I'd do whatever he wanted. He liked the fucking but would rather die than admit it. I wasn't going to admit it, either.

I went on, "What are you gonna do when they catch you? Ever been to jail before?"

"Shut up," he hissed.

"I bet you have," I said. "I bet you broke out cause once they got a guy like you, they're gonna keep him for good."

He stared at me as if he couldn't believe I was saying these things to him. After all, he was an educated man. I knew it got to him, just implying someone like him would have ever been to jail. He thought he had me all figured out and here I was, all of a sudden, acting like a supreme bitch again.

"Shut it," he muttered dangerously. "You will do it tomorrow."

"No, you're wrong," I said.

The danger in his voice was now across his face. He was mad. Big deal. He liked being mad, it's probably all that knew, that one emotion that came from a deep rooted hostility at the entire world. This was all he knew, anger. I almost stopped myself but for some reason I didn't. Maybe I liked seeing how pissed off I could get him.

"I'm not doing anything," I said and put my feet up on the table. "You can leave now."

"Why don't you leave?" he asked.

"You know," I said. "I think I might."

I got up and started out of the room. He grabbed my arm and shook his head.

"You're not going anywhere," he said.

"But you told me to leave," I said and wriggled out of his grasp. "Isn't that what you want?"

"No," he said. "But you need to be taught a lesson."

"Huh?" I asked.

He didn't respond. He only grabbed my arm and dragged me through the house. I yelled at him that this was getting a little old but he wouldn't let me go. So, I just let myself be dragged and then he took me into my bedroom and threw me on the bed.

I jumped up. "Oh, no, buddy, we're not doing this again."

Not one word came out of his mouth. He just turned on his heel and left the room. He came back in with a rope. I blinked. Uh oh.

"No!" I screeched and jumped up off the bed.

He grabbed me and wrestled me back to the bed. I slapped at him and tried to claw his face but the held me down and in no time had my arms and legs tied. I hadn't expected this. I was almost scared. But something inside me told me that no matter how far we went, he would never really hurt me. I prayed that instinct was correct.

After he had secured the ropes, he turned and started out of the room. *Bastard!* I tried to get the ropes free but it was no use. He must have taken a rope-tying class or something.

He glanced over his shoulder then stopped, standing stock still for a moment. My heart, which was already racing, sped up. The hesitation he had made me realize he wasn't finished. What was he going to do? But then I knew and knowing made me want it.

112

His eyes were all over my body making me feel—and want to be—naked. My nipples hardened under his intense gaze. I felt myself grow warm, wet. Just because he *looked* at me like that. He couldn't deny his desire for me. That look told on him. He wanted me as much as I denied wanting him, maybe even more so. I could be wrong but I had a feeling I was right.

Suddenly, the ropes didn't matter. It didn't matter that I was tied up, almost enslaved. Nothing mattered but the look on his face. I stopped struggling, stopped trying to get the ropes free. I just stared at him and waited.

He came over to the bed and continued to stare at me. Then he began to unbutton the dress until it came apart and fell away from my body. I didn't have any underwear on. I hadn't worn any since I'd gotten here mainly because I hadn't packed a bag.

I was uncovered, naked. He didn't look away from me, or my nakedness. He just stared. He wasn't looking at me so much as a human but as a woman. He was man and this was the way he was supposed to look at me, with lust, pure unadulterated lust and desire. It wasn't something a person could fake.

The lust was building inside of me. I had to have him do something. I moaned, arching, wanting his hands badly. I wanted him to paw at me and to use me because, in turn, I'd get to use him.

It took a long time before he began to play with me. One finger came down and I tensed. Before it reached my skin, I trembled and shivered. The anticipation was too much. His finger went to my belly and he traced a line from it down, where he traced another line through it until he was at pussy. I couldn't move my legs or arms. I had to lay there and enjoy the torture. I moaned again, this time more intensely. The finger came back up and lightly touched my nipples. He switched back and forth between them until I moaned for his lips to be on them.

He bent over and his tongue came out and he licked my nipple, sucked it into his mouth and bit down gently on it. I moaned more loudly. It was too much. I couldn't contain myself. He began to nibble on my breast and his hand was between my legs sideways, going up and down and it felt so good I couldn't control myself. All I had to do was lay there and let it happen. I didn't force the orgasm to come; it came on its own. It came quickly and sporadically until I was spent and trembling.

He didn't stop there. He began to kiss my body, all of it, my face and my legs, everywhere he kissed and explored before he kissed me, his tongue forcing its way into my wet mouth. I moaned and sucked at his tongue and his hands kept moving. His dick was hard and I could feel it pressing against my leg. I wanted it inside me, filling me up, fucking me hard, fucking me like it didn't give a damn what or where as long as I stayed there until it got its satisfaction. Until it was finished with me.

The feeling of the ropes, the constriction swept over me. But then came a feeling of freedom, of release combined with beautiful pain. I wanted out but I wanted to stay put, to stay secure. There was so much security in being tied up. It was all up to him, what to do and how to do it. I was just the willing vessel.

He didn't untie my legs. He slid his cock between them and pulled them open just enough so he could get in. He took his time and eased into me before he gave a good hard push and forced me to take it all.

He kissed me hard as he began to fuck me, grabbing my head and holding it still as he forced his tongue into my mouth. I kissed back but couldn't move. I had to take it, so I lay there all tied up, and took it, as he fucked me, as he brought the best out in me. It was getting to be too much; it was too good. I was panting and the orgasm inside me was building. Soon, it erupted and exploded.

I shuddered as it hit me and then stared into his eyes as I came. He stared back and I could tell he was about to come, too. He might have been using me, but it was me he wanted beneath him. It was him I wanted on top of me. No one else would do. It was like I had found my place in the world and my place was with him.

The orgasm held on and intensified, which made me pant more. He pulled back and began to pump into me harder. As the good feelings wash all over me, I watched his face. I loved to watch his face as he came. His face had such a look of concentration when he came. I loved that look.

Once we were done, he fell beside me, breathing heavily. Then he turned and looked at me. I turned and looked back, wondering what he was thinking, but then realizing I knew. The look he had was almost hopeless, like he had lost something and, while it made him sad, he was glad to have lost it. In its place, something better had come along.

I knew exactly how he felt.

"He knew it drove me crazy."
From *Dead Sexy: Two Tales of Vampire Erotica,
Book One—Breathe*.

*The setup: After Lola and Hugo go hunting, they go
back to their place for a nightcap of a different kind.*

The hunt was the least favorite part of the night. For me, I mean. Hugo loved it. But then again, he'd come to love it as any normal vampire would. It's just that I wasn't a normal vampire.

Hugo and I sat at the bar and waited for the victim to arrive. It was getting late and we were both starving. The red wine glasses were almost empty and the bartender was getting tired. The crowd was thinning out and Hugo was getting slightly agitated. But then he was horny too. He always got so horny and alive before a kill.

I tried not to think about that.

I tried not to think about that as I felt his hand move up my arm and then push the hair away from my neck before his lips came to rest on the skin just below my ear. He gave me a long, slow kiss before pulling away, standing and then walking off. His hand came out towards me and I stood, taking it as I stared at the man in the booth who I knew was going to be our victim. He was an older man and he was staring at us intently. He was wondering what it would be like to be Hugo, who, he was sure, was taking me home to fuck me.

I stared at the man as I walked out, stared at him until he looked into my eyes. And once he did, he immediately rose and followed us. We walked slowly, with purpose, out the door and onto the street. I turned around to see the man following closely at our heels. I turned back around and held fast to Hugo's hand. He squeezed my hand then ducked into an alley as I walked on.

I never heard or saw a thing.

I walked about a block, then turned back around and went back to the alley. Hugo nodded at me and I got on my knees next to the man, who was now only barely alive. I avoided his heavy-lidded eyes and the sun spots on his hands. I didn't think about who this man was or the children—and grandchildren—he might have. Hugo went in for the blood that would feed me. I didn't watch as he did it. But as soon as he turned to me, I opened my mouth and the man's blood trickled in. Once I felt that rush of blood, of life, a sense of calm and purpose came over me.

Hugo kept doing this until I was full. Then he finished the man off. When he was done, he stood, took my hand and we walked away.

This was the way it was. This was the way it had been for a while. But all that was about to change.

"Do you know how truly beautiful you are, Lola?" he asked me later that night.

I nodded and smiled a little. He made me feel so beautiful that it didn't embarrass me to agree. I felt no shame from the compliment. I never felt shame around him—ever. My hair was long and dark and my eyes were blue, crystal clear blue. My skin was subtle and as undamaged as a baby's. My body was ripe for the taking, small and delicate, petite but with a nice ass and a great set of breasts, which he loved to devour.

"You are," he said, staring at me. "You are truly beautiful."

Through the eyes of our lovers, we see time. We see ourselves standing in it, standing in time, being ourselves and being loved for just that. That is what we crave. That's the way I saw him, for who he really was. That's the way he said he saw me. Innocent but hurt, craving something. He wanted to give me that something I needed that neither of us could name.

"You don't fool me," I told him once. "You're evil."

"That I am, love," he said, giving me a sheepish grin. "But then again, so are you."

And I was. Evil. It was strange to say, strange to be, evil. But I was evil. I was as evil as he was. He had made me that way. He had destroyed me, only to bring me back from the dead, to the living. That's where I was now. Before him, I'd not been myself, not been the person or thing I was supposed to be. I had always been alone, unfulfilled. He had made me feel, he had made me full. He made me into the thing I was now. I was finally whole.

And now he was giving me that look again. That look that told me it was time to submit and to allow him to take me over. It was time, the look said, for me to lie down and take what he was going to give. I tensed in anticipation, tensed almost with fear. Our love making was always violent, despite the fact that it could be sweet and controlled. We liked it rough, though, and when we were done, we would survey the marks on our bodies that would heal almost as soon as they appeared. We would be proud of the marks, proud of our insatiable appetite for each other. Proud that we could bring that animal out.

The sex was the best I'd ever had in my entire life. It was addicting, the sex, and the more I had, the more I wanted. It was more fun in the beginning, when he didn't look so remorseful.

Sometimes, he would tie me up just to let me go. I would lie there and anticipate his next move. I would lie there and watch him watching me. He loved to stare at me, at my naked body. He loved to hold back and make me squirm, make me beg for it. And I'd beg. I'd do anything to get it. That's how good it made me feel. It made me feel so good I'd act like a fool, like a complete fool, just to have it again, just to feel him so close to me. He made me feel so alive, so free, so uninhibited, so insatiable. All the things in the world I'd been missing before I met him, I felt. I felt them so much I sometimes wondered how I used to feel and that emptiness would always threaten to fill me again. But as long as he made me feel like this, as long as he stayed around, I'd be okay. I'd be fine as long as he made me feel like I was meant to feel.

Just as he was making me feel now.

Now he was all mine. He was giving me the look. The look told me I was the sexiest creature he'd ever come in contact with. The look told me he wasn't going to move one inch until I gave him the signal.

"Go ahead," I said. "Do it."

He grinned at me. I smiled back from my position on the bed, which I was tied to. I couldn't move. Well, I could have if I had wanted to. I was strong, so strong that I never had to find myself in a position where I had to submit to anyone. I could tug at the rope just a little and it'd break. I could get away if I wanted to. But I didn't want to. All I wanted to do was tell him what I wanted and what I wanted was to be fucked. Fucked good.

He bent over me, over my naked body, and ran his head up and down it, nuzzling me. I began to feel it, to feel warm. This was the best part, the anticipation. Without it, I couldn't go on to do the things we were going to do.

He began to run his hands over my body, stopping to fondle my breasts. I rose up from the bed at that, wanting his lips on my nipples, wanting him on top of me. But not so soon. He kept his hands moving as he stared at me from the corner of his eye. He was watching me again. He loved to watch.

"What now?" he asked softly.

"Touch me," I said. "Touch me there."

"Where?" he asked and slid his hand between my legs. "There?"

I squeezed my eyes shut and nodded. It felt so good as he touched and explored me down there. No inch was left uncovered, undiscovered. He moved his hand a little and found my spot. I moaned loudly and licked my lips. It was too much, it was too good. I had to have it, though. I would have died if I didn't.

His hand stayed still and I began to move against it, using it to get off, to come. He bent down and nibbled at me, licking and pushing his head between my legs. My legs began to part and invited him in to taste me. So he did. He tasted me, licked at me and within seconds, I was erupting with pleasure, with orgasm, with pure and total delight.

Then he was on top of me, kissing me, giving me himself. As he kissed me, I began to respond and kiss back, harder, wanting him inside of me. His mouth found my nipple and began to suck greedily at it, grabbing at it and squeezing as he gave me pleasure. I wished my hands were free to explore him, so I jerked on the ropes and they broke, leaving my hands untied. My arms encircled him and squeezed tight. He moaned as my hands went down his back and to his ass and there they squeezed. My hands came back up and held his head still so I could kiss him and lick at his lips.

His lips ate at mine as if he were starving. And he was. He was starving with lust for me. He couldn't get enough of my lips or of me. I loved having that power over him to bring him to the point of no return.

"Now," I said, looking into his eyes. "Do it now."

Without a word, he complied and pushed my legs open with his knee. His body settled between my legs and I felt his hard cock on my leg before I felt it pushing inside of me.

I moaned as soon as he was all the way in. We were complete now, two pieces to the puzzle, solved. We were one together, one alone, one person, one being, and one thing. It was just me and him, us against the world, us alone in ours.

His mouth was back on top of mine as he began to fuck me, take me over, control me. I sucked at his lips, loving the way his skin felt against mine. Then we began to move together, move as one. Our eyes opened and we stared intensely at one another, almost smiling. This is what we liked best. It was the best in us, giving it to each other.

He began to fuck me, really fuck me, which sent me over the edge, which made me beg and moan for him to do it, to do it harder, to take me, to ravish me. He loved doing this to me. He knew it drove me crazy, wild. I loved having it done to me. I loved fucking him. I loved him, it was that simple.

It took us over then. We were only participants, caught up in the mood, in the love. We were overcome with passion and all we could do was hang on and ride it out. Our eyes were filled with lust for one another and our loins craved each other. There was nothing left to do but come and come we did. We came hard, slamming into each other, taking what we could and consuming it greedily. I was panting and I was shivering with delight and then I was done.

So was he.

We didn't say a word afterwards. There wasn't really much we could have said. The intensity of it spoke for itself. He only settled on the bed beside me and took me in his arms. He stared into my eyes before he touched the side of my face with his hand.

"You know I love you, right?" he asked.

I smiled and said, "And I love you, too."

He nodded, kissed my cheek and then closed his eyes. I stared at the window. It was morning, daylight, and it was time for rest. I closed my eyes, too.

"The hot intensity of it."
From *Dead Sexy: Two Tales of Vampire Erotica, Book One—Breathe*.

The setup: Lola recalls the times she had with Hugo, the good and the bad.

The chase continued but it was becoming harder and harder to keep up with him. He became an obsession to me. He became the hunted, but was I really hunting myself? Had the witch been right? Was this all about my insecurity, my inability to face up to the truth? Was I deluding myself into believing in something that might not have been there from the beginning? I didn't know and at that point, I didn't really care. All I knew was that I had to find him.

I chased him through most of the South. Through the Carolinas and then down to Florida, even to Miami. I was sure he'd go on to Key West just to piss me off because it was always so hot and sunny there. But then his direction changed and I lost him, once again.

This began to get really old.

I kept on, as only a woman scorned can. I kept the chase up, hot on his heels, just missing him everywhere I went. But I didn't even think about giving up. Giving up wasn't in my blood or in my ability when it came to Hugo. I was going to finish this one way or another.

As I chased, as I drove that old, worn-out car, crisscrossing the South, I would think of us, how we'd been together, how we'd loved. I would think about the good times, the happy times, then I'd think about the sex, the hot intensity of it, its animalistic nature. There were many things I remembered—the coolness of his skin as I pressed myself against him, the sharpness of his teeth as he nibbled on my nipple, the power of his eyes as he took me.

After a kill, he'd be especially ready to give me all he had. He would push himself deep down into me. He would savor me, take me. He could do anything and everything he wanted to do to me and I would beg for it. He would tie me up, he would take me down. I went willingly, all for the sex, all for the pleasure.

And now missing that pleasure in my life was tormenting me. I still wanted him, still needed him. Why did I have to need him like that? He was so strong and I relied on his strength much more than I'd allowed myself to believe. He was stronger than me, even when I drained him of all his power.

There was one time when I'd almost taken all the blood he had. I'd sucked so hard on his arm, loving the feeling of his blood mingling with mine, that I had to have it. I couldn't stop. He had to throw me away from him but I went right back in, trying to get the blood, trying to drain every ounce from him and put it into me.

"Get off!" he hissed and pushed me away.

"Give it to me!" I screamed once and tried to hit him.

He dodged me and shook his head. "Try it, Lola, and see me tear you from limb to limb."

Maybe that's what I couldn't stand, the thought that he was so much stronger than me. Maybe I thought I could take his power if I drained him of all his blood. Maybe I thought I could somehow be more like him if I had it all. *Give it to me! Give me the blood! Make me whole!*

I tried again. He pushed me away from him, more gently than before, and shook his head at me.

"That's your last warning, Lola."

"Then don't do this to me," I cried. "Don't do this!"

"Do what?" he asked softly and walked over to me.

"Bring those people in here and suck them dry," I said. "Don't bring them here. Do it somewhere else. I can't stand their smell!"

He chuckled and shook his head at me, which infuriated me even more.

"I can't do this," I said. "I just can't. Please don't bring anyone else into our house again."

"You'll get weak," he said, bending down to stare into my eyes. "*Weak*. Slowly you'll shrivel and become skin and bones but you won't die. You'll just be a husk. All your beauty will be lost. Is that what you want, Lola?"

"You know it isn't," I hissed and before I could stop myself, I had slapped him across the mouth.

His head shot to the side and his lip bled. Then he turned on me and his eyes seemed to light up. I was almost frightened, almost scared and started to back away from him. I didn't get the chance. He threw me across the room. I fell with a thud and became infuriated. I got right back up and was at him. We attacked each other, each trying to bring the other down. And he won, as he always did. I succumbed and began to lick and kiss at his mouth, which was stained red from the blood he'd just consumed.

"Give it to me," I moaned and grabbed onto his cock. "Give it all to me, baby. Now!"

"Like this?" he asked and began to push me up against the wall.

"Oh, yeah," I said as he grabbed my breasts. "Fuck me."

I didn't have to tell him twice. He had the clothes, literally, ripped from my body in an instant and he was filling me up, consuming me. I loved to be consumed by him, to take it all, to give it back. We were alone then, as we always were. Our foreheads pressed up against the others and our eyes never wavered for a second. He was taking me and I liked being taken.

He drove it in harder and I gasped from the pain, from the pleasure. He was the best I'd ever had and he had it all—he had the looks and the intensity and the "don't mess with me" attitude, which made me want to mess with him even more, of course. He set the fire in my heart and he stoked it, just like he was stoking me, as he was taking me. It was too much and I was too turned on and before I could stop myself, I threw my head back and moaned loudly with the orgasm as it swept though my body, as it gave me peace and understanding. And what I understood was simple. He had my heart. He had all of me, probably always would.

I didn't mind that one bit.

"Oh, there, don't stop, right there…"
From *Dead Sexy: Two Tales of Vampire Erotica,
Book Two—I Married a Vampire.*

*The setup: Even though Keri and Duke are newlyweds,
they still like to spice things up in the bedroom. Or, rather,
out of it.*

I was leaving work late, as usual. It was Thursday and
the security guard stopped and asked if I would like him to
walk me to my car.

"No, thanks," I said and smiled. "I'll be fine."

He nodded. "Be careful."

"Will do," I replied and walked out into the dark
Atlanta night. I walked down to the street corner and
pressed the "walk" button and waited. Just as the light
changed, I heard something behind me. I looked around and
studied the dark alley. There was nothing there. I turned
back to the light and hurried across the street before it
changed.

After I got to the other side and was nearing the parking
garage, I definitely heard something behind me. I stopped
and looked and could have sworn I saw someone duck into a
doorway. I suddenly became aware of my surroundings and
became very nervous. I hurried up. The parking garage was
only a few yards away. I heard the noise again and increased
my pace, almost into a jog. I looked behind me and saw a
man, a tall, dark man and he was coming after me. No, he
was coming *for* me and he was going to do God knows what.

I wished I had let the security guard walk me to my car.

My fight or flight instinct took over and I ran as fast as I
could up the street, even though I was wearing heels and it
was difficult. I soon forgot about the car and just focused on

trying to find an unlocked building or a person who could help me. I looked behind me to see that he was gaining on me. I screamed. He got closer and chased me down a dark alley and there I came to a dead-end.

I turned around and faced him. He was glaring at me, as if he had a personal vendetta against me. The way he looked at me made me feel as though he could tear me from limb to limb without a thought. And he probably could.

"Stay away from me!" I screamed and rummaged in my purse for my pepper spray, then held it on him. "Stay away!"

He disregarded my words and kept walking, very slowly, to where I stood. Then he knocked the pepper spray out of my hand. I shivered as he grabbed me. He was going to kill me.

"Please," I begged. "Don't do this. Please, I'll—"

"Shut up," he grunted.

I shut up and stared into his dark blue eyes and then at his body, his lean and muscular body. Why was a guy like this chasing girls? He could get a girl—any girl—he wanted. He didn't have to do this, so why was he?

Just then his face changed and it changed into this mean, weird looking thing. It was still his face, only more distorted, more vicious. He looked like a monster. Then I realized that he *was* a monster! As I studied him closer I could see the fangs in his mouth, sharp to the touch, ready to sink into my throat and suck the life's blood out of me.

"Oh, God!" I screamed. "OH GOD!"

He grinned evilly and then shook his head and the monster face disappeared and was replaced by his other face, the handsome face. That terrified me more than the other face and that was because it was deceptive.

He leaned in and pressed his cold lips against mine. I struggled as he tried to kiss me. I beat against his chest and pushed him away but there wasn't much I could do but give in. And, as I submitted, I felt relief wash over me and I felt something else, too. I wanted this and I wanted it more than I'd ever wanted anything in my life. I wanted what he was going to do to me next but the thought didn't disturb me. It just propelled me into the next moment.

My lips softened and he began to kiss me, eat at my lips, suck on them. His hand was under my skirt and he was ripping the panties from my body. I tried to get away but then I didn't want to. He was touching me, playing with me, teasing me, making me want it. And want it, I did. I wanted it so badly, even if I had to take it from him.

"Don't," I said but didn't mean it as he began to suck at my throat. "Please stop."

He didn't respond and continued to lick and suck at my throat and then he ripped my shirt open and devoured my breasts. He flicked his tongue across my nipple before sucking it into his mouth. He squeezed my breast with one hand while the other was between my legs, playing with my pussy. I couldn't take much more of this. I was going to explode with orgasm if he didn't stop. *I was going to... Oh, there, don't stop, right there... I was going to...I was going to heaven.* I had to have it. I had to have his finger on me, teasing me, bringing out the best I had. And then I had it. I exploded with orgasm and it took my breath away. And then, when it was over, I wanted more where that came from.

"Oh, God!" I moaned. "Fuck me!"

He pushed me up against the wall and I wrapped my legs around his waist and he shoved his hard cock into me and started to fuck me. I sucked him into me and rode him like he was riding me. I couldn't get enough of him, of this moment; even if it was wrong, it felt right. It felt right to have him do that to me, to fuck me in an alley. *What would he do after we were done?*

128

I began to come right then, as he was coming. I couldn't get enough of it and wanted it so bad, just like I wanted him. The orgasm exploded inside me and I threw my head back and screamed with delight, almost with pain because it was so good it was almost unbearable.

"Oh, yeah," he said. "Oh God!"

I met him as he pumped into me and fucked that orgasm right out of his body. We kept fucking until he was spent and I could barely move.

"Umm," he moaned and kissed me gently, sliding his tongue over my lips before he pushed it into my mouth. He pulled away and smiled at me.

"Oh, baby," I moaned and grinned back. "That was so good."

"It was, wasn't it?" he asked and seemed pleased with himself.

"Do the scary face again!" I exclaimed.

He groaned. "Oh, come on, Keri."

"*Please!*" He groaned again and did it. Oh! He was *so* scary when he did that. And so sexy. I touched the bottom of his teeth and said, "How do you keep them so sharp?"

"I don't have to keep them sharp, they just stay that way," he said and shook his head, going back to his normal face.

"Oh," I said. "Next time I want you to chase me in the park and we can have sex on a bench."

"Can't we just do it in a bed every once in a while?"

I studied him and replied, "What's the fun in that?"

"He always knew what to say."
From *Dead Sexy: Two Tales of Vampire Erotica, Book Two—I Married a Vampire*.

The setup: Keri likes to please her vampire in more ways than one.

"You are so sexy," Duke said. "Dead sexy."

I smiled at him. He was on the couch waiting for me. I loved making him wait.

"Oh, damn," he said. "You look hot."

The good thing about being a newlywed was that the sex was never boring. Also, I enjoyed dressing up and turning my vampire on. I smiled at him and leaned against the wall. He stared at me intently, his eyes not wavering from my body at all. He liked my schoolgirl outfit and the fact that my hair was in braids. He liked the penny loafers and bobby socks, too. He liked me looking like a hot schoolgirl.

"Come here," he said and motioned me over.

"Where?" I teased and pointed. "Over there?"

"Yes, over here," he said.

I bit my bottom lip and walked over to him and got between his legs like a stripper. He smiled at me and I smiled back a little, then ran my hands up and down his legs, slightly scraping my nails against his pants. I suddenly felt a surge of power and that enabled me to really get into it. It enabled me to give my body over to the act of giving my man pleasure. I began to lean in towards him with my whole body, grinding it against his crotch.

His hands were all over me as I moved against him. He wanted me, he wanted to fuck me, but he wanted me to be a little tease first. I was going to give him what he wanted and I was going to torture him beforehand.

I ran my head up and down his body like a cat and he responded by grabbing it and kissing me. We ate at each other's mouths for a moment, taking turns to suck at our tongues and lips. It was a wet, hot intense kiss and got me so hot I wanted to eat him alive. Or dead. Or whatever.

I moved away from his mouth and kissed his face, all of it, even his eyelids, then slid my tongue along his throat before I sucked it. Then I was going down, down towards his cock which was ready and hard, sticking up inside of his pants, forming a tent.

I nibbled and kissed my way down and stuck my head between his legs and started to nibble on his crotch. I took my time to tease him. It worked because a loud moan soon came out of his mouth. He was getting excited. He was losing himself in it. That made me feel strong and sexy.

"Oh, baby," he moaned. "Just put it in your mouth."

I grinned because I had him, literally, by the balls. I unzipped his pants and his dick popped out. It was in my hands and it was long and hard, slightly throbbing as it awaited my mouth. It was ready for me to do what I was going to do, ready to please me if I decided I wanted that. But this was his turn and he was going to get what he wanted.

"You are so hot," he said and ran his hands through my hair.

"Mmm," I moaned.

I rose up and gave him a big, open-mouthed kiss, sucking at his lips before I began to give him a hand job. I gripped it and ran my hands up and down it, lightly fingering the shaft. He moaned and nearly rose up off the

131

couch. I ignored him and concentrated only on his dick, running my hands up and down it, gripping it like a baseball bat.

"That's a little tight," he said. "Ease up just a little."

I eased up and gave him a lighter stroke. He responded by nodding and looking at me like I was the only woman on earth. I *loved* that.

I stared up at him as I stroked and he stared down at me. There was such sexual tension in that stare, it was unbelievable. Such pure sexual energy. It was almost beautiful.

It was time to really get the show on the road. I dropped my mouth to it then and he grunted as my lips made first contact. I went up and down on it, using my hands to grip it as I sucked. The saliva from my mouth made it easier. It was all wet and sexy. Then I forgot about everything else and deep-throated him, then sucked him harder.

He came up off the couch.

"Shh," I said. "Sit still."

"It's hard to," he muttered.

I shook my head at him and went right back down on it, all the way to the end and then back up, again, sucking as hard as I could. I came up for some air, keeping my hands stroking him and said, "Do you like that?"

"It's the best thing in the world, baby," he murmured. "The best feeling in the world."

I grinned and went back down on it, then came back up and said, "It tastes good."

He grinned and nodded. "It feels good, too."

"Mmm," I moaned, sucking it. "Your cock tastes so good, baby."

I was really into it, so much that I was making all kinds of strange noises as I sucked. I realized I was so turned on, I wanted him to fuck me. But not before I was done with this.

I wanted to complete this mission. I wanted to give him something he would *never* forget.

I was having such a good time, I didn't even realize he was about to come. It was all about me giving it to him and getting pleasure from giving. I knew he liked the way I sucked him. I sucked him hard, like I was sucking a lollipop. I was sucking him so hard he was wriggling. He was moaning. He was about to come.

But before I let him come, I totally lost all inhibition. I raised his cock up and licked my way down it to his balls and then I sucked them into my mouth, gently sucking them as I knew too much pressure would hurt him.

"Fuck!" he moaned. "Fuck!"

I gave his balls one last suck, then went back to his cock. I couldn't believe he was still holding it. Maybe because I hadn't told him he could come yet. I was in control. He wasn't about to do anything until I said to.

"Come on now, baby," I said softly. "Come on."

He nodded and I went back to his cock. As I gave one last, hard suck, he erupted and came into my mouth, his white hot cum filling it up. I swallowed and kept sucking until he was dry. I felt some of his cum on the side of my mouth. I licked the corner of my mouth and stared up at him. He stared down at me with an intense look of shock and wonder. I never felt so alive as I did, so loved and so worshipped. He was going to worship me from now on. He would be out of his mind with lust for me from now on. I had him and that was a good feeling.

"I can't believe you just did that," he said in awe. "You are so fantastic."

I grinned and climbed up on him, pushing him back on the couch. I said, "Now your turn."

He grinned back and grabbed me, kissing me so hard I lost my breath. Then his hand began to roam my body, tearing at my clothes until I was completely and totally naked. He flipped us over until I was beneath him and he was back in control. I just lay there and panted, knowing what was coming and wanting it so bad I couldn't take it. I prayed he wouldn't stop.

He didn't. He began to finger me, rubbing me lightly before he pushed one finger inside of me. I arched up and moaned loudly. He kept his thumb on my clit and kept moving it in circles.

"You are so wet," he said and kissed me. "So hot, baby."

I smiled at him. He smiled back and began to kiss his way down my body until he was between my legs and there he pushed his head in and gave me one long and hot lick. I grabbed at his head and wanted more. He gave it to me and began to suck at my entire pussy, using the long strokes I loved. He kept at it until I was moaning with each breath. He didn't move away from me until I grabbed his head and pushed myself into his face, begging him not to stop. I was coming hard and it was a powerful orgasm that took over my entire being. I felt like I was on fire.

"Oh, God, oh, yes," I moaned and grabbed at his dick which was, thankfully, hard again. (That's one good thing about being married to a vampire—they can go all night.) I moaned and wriggled, then shouted, "Fuck me!"

He was on top of me, fucking me, taking me. Using me as I used him. We couldn't have stopped for anything; we were that turned on. I wrapped my legs around his waist and pushed him in as deep as he could get. I felt totally connected with him then; it was just us, fucking and giving each other a pleasure that's unattainable except for an act like this.

But then it hit me, the second orgasm, and I grabbed onto him and sunk my teeth into his shoulder. He cried out, not with pain, but from pleasure, as he came with me. We were slamming into each other, fucking so hard the couch rocked.

"Oh, God," I moaned as I shook with the orgasm. "OH, GOD!"

He grunted and slammed into me a few more times just as my orgasm began to dissipate. Then it was over. He fell on top of me and caught his breath. It took me a few seconds to get my breath back. As I lay there panting, I looked over at him and said, "You're a dirty vamp."

He grinned at me and said, "And you're a dirty girl."

I smiled, very pleased with myself.

He nuzzled my neck and said softly, "That was the best, baby."

I nodded. Yeah. I knew it.

He kissed my cheek. "Thanks."

"You're welcome," I said, then stared at the bite mark I'd left on his shoulder. "Sorry about that."

He glanced at it. "That's okay. In fact, that was hot."

I nodded. "It looks like a vamp bite, doesn't it?"

He shrugged. "Well, it's in the wrong place, but yeah, I guess. A little."

"I'd make a good vampire," I said and kissed the mark.

He stared at me.

"I'd be so hot, I'd be smoking," I said and grinned evilly. "Why don't you turn me?"

"What?"

"Into a vampire," I said. "It would be great, just us two, being vamps. Besides that, I wouldn't have to worry about wrinkles or—"

"Don't you ever say that again," he said angrily.

"Why?" I asked, sitting up.

He glared at me and got up.

"What is it?" I asked.

"You have no idea what kind of pain you have to go through to become a vampire, do you? It can kill people, it's that bad. Plus, you might turn all evil. You might go bad, you know? Not everyone turns out like me."

I scoffed. "Please. Like you're so strong and so good."

"That's not what I meant," he said. "If you died, I'd die."

"Huh?"

He looked away. "Keri, do you know how much I love you? And if I turned you and you died, I'd want to die."

"How sweet," I said and threw my hands around his neck.

"I mean it," he said. "Don't ever mention me turning you again."

"Fine," I grumbled. "But what about when I get old and ugly? You'll still be young and hot."

"You'll never be old or ugly," he said.

"How's that?"

"Because you'll always be beautiful to me even when you're old and ugly."

"You say that now but just wait until my tits sag," I said. "I'm thirty-four, almost thirty-five, now. It might not be long before these puppies head south."

His head jerked up. He hadn't thought about that.

"See?" I said and pointed my finger at him. "And when I'm gone, you can get another girl and live another life. It's not really fair when you get right down to it."

He grabbed my finger and shook his head. "When you croak, I croak."

"Huh?"

"When you die," he said. "I'm going to off myself."

"You said that before," I said. "Are you really serious about this?"

He nodded. "I don't want to live without you."

I grinned at him. He was so good with that stuff. He always knew what to say.

Then he said, "What's for supper?"

I groaned.

Lightning Source UK Ltd.
Milton Keynes UK
UKOW051455300412

191747UK00001B/88/A